Books by Richard Helms

Geary's Year
Geary's Gold
The Valentine Profile
The Amadeus Legacy
Joker Poker
Voodoo That You Do
Juicy Watusi
Wet Debt
Naked Came the Flamingo (contributor)
Paid In Spades
Bobby J.
Grass Sandal
Cordite Wine
The Daedalus Deception
The Unresolved Seventh
The Mojito Coast
Six Mile Creek
Thunder Moon
Older Than Goodbye
Brittle Karma
Doctor Hate

RICHARD HELMS

DOCTOR HATE

an Eamon Gold novel

BLACK ARCH BOOKS

For Elaine

Cor meum in aeternum

ONE

Brandon Hunt sat across from me in my office. He was slim, well-dressed, and appeared to have an open, inviting face—at least the part of it I could see that wasn't bandaged. I was reminded of the cautions against judging books by covers.

"I'm told there won't be any permanent scars, Mr. Gold," he said, as if he had read my thoughts.

"Well," I said, "There's that."

"They were lying in wait for me on the way to parking lot."

"How many?" I asked.

"Four. Maybe five."

"Can you describe them?"

"No. They put a bag or a towel or something over my head before they laid into me."

"Pity."

"I don't hear a lot of empathy in your voice," Hunt said.

"Still gathering information. Empathy costs extra."

"What do you charge?"

I told him. He winced a little. Then I told him that number didn't include expenses. I think I ruined his day. I pulled a sheaf of printouts from my desk drawer.

"After you called for an appointment, I did some research," I said. "You're kind of famous, Doctor Hunt."

"Do you run background checks on all your potential clients, Gold?"

I noted he'd dropped the '*Mister*'. We were making progress on revealing the genuine Brandon Hunt.

"As a matter of fact, I do," I said. "Usually it's just a credit check, but…"

"You checked my credit? Do you have any idea what that will do to my rating?"

"Have you seen your face? Priorities. When I started the check, I found over ten thousand hits on various search engines. You should be glad I don't charge by the hour for that. You've been a busy boy."

"If I were black and you called me that, I could ruin your life."

"You could try. This is you, right?"

I passed the papers to him. He glanced at them, without touching them, and waved his hand in the air.

"Sure, that's me. What about it?"

I picked up the top sheet. It was a string of Twitter posts.

"You have a curious nickname," I said. "A lot of the junior pundits on Twitter refer to you as Doctor Hate. On October twelfth, you said, '*Sick and tired of seeing so much money spent on Women's Studies. Where is the Men's Studies program? After all, the only thing women want to really study is men*'."

"So?"

"You don't find that attitude a little…archaic?" I asked. "Especially here in San Francisco?"

"I'm entitled to my opinion. Same as you."

"And this one? '*Wish my Middle Eastern students wouldn't sit on the front row in class. I can't see people raising their hands over all the turbans.*'"

"I'm not the only professor who's ever said that."

"You're the only one I've heard say it in public. During the Black Lives Matter protests last year, you wrote, '*What are all these people doing in the street? Why aren't they at home, watching* Madea *movies, making babies and collecting welfare checks?*' Kind of inflammatory, wasn't it?"

"What's your point?" Hunt said. "I'm a conservative. I have a point of view, and I'm allowed to express it. Even the university said so."

"What they said, in essence, was that your public statements are embarrassing, inexcusable, and unrepresentative of university values and mission, but they are protected by the First Amendment, and your tenured status makes it impossible for them to dump you just because you're a jerk, a racist, a sexist pig, and a xenophobic asshole." I paused, for effect. "*Professor,*" I added.

Hunt leaned back in his chair and held up both hands. "Is this a great fucking country or what? And, believe me, they tried to get rid of me. More than once."

"That's why you took them to court?"

"Naw. I took them to court for denying me tenure in the first place. And I won. I was due, Gold. I'd earned it. My political and social beliefs are immaterial compared to my record of published research."

"That would be the research in which you attempt to scientifically demonstrate that minorities are intellectually inferior to whites?"

"I never did any such thing. I went where my data took me. What are you, a fucking prosecuting attorney? I got the shit beat out of me the other night. I need protection."

"Assault and battery are crimes. You need the police, not a private investigator."

"They took their report. Said they'd look into it. Want to know exactly how long they spent taking prints and samples from the scene where I got beat down? Less time than it took to speak that sentence. They aren't going to do shit."

"Perhaps you shouldn't have referred to them as *undereducated crossing guards* in one of your Twitter screeds," I suggested.

"Those were the campus cops. You know—the guys who couldn't get into the regular police academy because they rode the short bus to elementary school."

"Cops are a fraternity. They hang together. You stick it to one, you're taking on the entire Thin Blue Line. I'll hand it to you, though. You're an equal opportunity offender. You insult and demean everyone."

"Are you going to take my case or what?" he asked. "I have a class in a half hour."

"What is it exactly you want me to do?" I asked.

"I'd like you to find out who beat me up, so I can charge them."

I shook my head. "It's an open police case. That's No Man's Land."

"Okay. Lacking that, I need protection. I checked up on you, too. You're good friends with Earleen Marley in my department at the university."

"You know Earleen?"

"Believe it or not, we're friends. She's appalled that I was attacked, and she said you were very, very good at what you do. The best, she said."

"My blushes," I said. "Hold on."

I picked up my phone and punched Earleen's office number in the directory. She answered on the second ring.

"Eamon," she said. "Thought I might hear from you."

"There's a gentleman in my office I'd just as soon chuck out the window into the bay," I said.

"So, Brandon Hunt contacted you."

"He did. Tell me why I should take his case."

"You shouldn't. I never referred him to you. He casually asked me who the best private eye in town was. I told him. He ran with that. I say this as his friend. Brandon's an asshole, Eamon. He taints almost everything that touches him."

"Right now, he's an asshole in danger," I said.

"Brandon's always in some trouble or another. You know about the petition to remove him?"

"I read about it online this afternoon."

"It's up to fifty thousand signatures across the state already. A lot of people are angry at Brandon and want to see him in a different line of work. Something involving sewers or potential falls from great heights."

"Won't the university have to respond to them eventually?"

"Can't. Won't. Boy's got tenure. Unless he's busted with a pound of cocaine, a naked dwarf clown, and a promiscuous goat in his car, he can say anything he wants."

"And does."

"And does. The university isn't going to fire him. They're educators, Eamon, not social warriors. They're spineless. Scared to death he'll take them to court again. But, you know what?"

"What?"

"He's not really a bad guy, underneath all that Junior Hitler shit. And he's scared. After that beatdown the other night, he's worried one of those petitioners might decide to do the university's job for them. I don't think you should take the job, but I think you will."

"You're going to need to explain that."

"You ever heard of a researcher named Sue?"

"I heard of a boy named Sue."

"Sue and his partners researched psychopathy. They stated that heroes and villains are just different sides of the same coin. Villains are ruthless when it comes to harming and destroying others. Heroes are ruthless when it comes to protecting others."

"Like the Joker and Batman."

"Exactly. Very perceptive. That's exactly the example I use in my classes. In this equation, you're Batman."

"Bullshit. I'm a meat and potatoes blue collar private cop. I live client to client. I only got an education because I wanted to play football."

"But you got that education. You do everything you set your mind to. I didn't send Brandon to you, and I wouldn't, because you're a buddy and I don't like to put buddies in bad situations. But if you take the case, I think you can help him."

I thanked her and placed my phone back on the desk.

"You're a fucking fraud," Hunt said.

"Butter me up some more," I told him. "Earleen had me ninety percent convinced to take your case. You're about to blow it."

"I'm a psychologist. I know people. You're nowhere near as dumb as you pretend to be. Earleen says you're the best there is. Revel in that! Brag about it! Your false humility is sickening. It's like white guilt, feeling awful for shit that happened two hundred years before you were born. This city's lousy with weenies like you."

"Were you born without social filters, or did they just scrape off along the way?"

He sat back and grinned.

"You were jerking me around," I said.

"Wanted to see if you could take it."

"Not a matter of can or can't. What matters is whether I want to."

"And?"

"I'm on the fence."

"You have other cases?"

"No, but I've had a good year. My bank account is bursting at the seams. And a nice, easy philandering spouse case is always just around the corner."

"Don't you get tired of sitting outside tawdry motels waiting for some cheater to walk out a door with his secretary? Seems to me this would be a nice change of pace. It's bodyguard work. You stand around and look like someone's going to toss you a raw steak. You're big, and wide, and kind of mean-looking. Just hang by my side, and nobody will bother me. We don't even have to talk if you like—not that I think we'd have much in common to discuss."

"I'll think about it. Call you tomorrow," I said.

TWO

When I first entered the private eye game, I signed on with an established guy named Dobbs. I'd been a cop on the San Francisco force, and eventually got my gold shield, but I was never terribly regimental in my habits, and as a result I decided to go private. Dobbs promised me a bright and successful future. We signed a contract, he took me on, and two weeks later he went nose-first into his plate at the Mark Hopkins. Aneurysm. Tough break for him. By the time his debts were paid, there wasn't enough to honor my contract, so his family instead offered me a rental property he'd bought on an impulse in Montara Beach, south of Pacifica on the PCH.

The house sits up the hill from the Chart House Restaurant, about four rows back from the highway. It's your standard central California beach house—shaggy redwood siding, crosshatched Tudor casement windows, a carport instead of a garage, two bedrooms, two baths, a kitchen, and a large living room. At first, I considered selling the place, but when I saw it, I discovered the living room would make a perfect workshop.

In addition to sleuthing, I'm a woodworker. I make stringed musical instruments—mostly guitars, but I've also made Irish citterns, a banjo or two, a Cuban cuatro, a few ukes, and most recently a hurdy-gurdy. I don't sell them, but I do give them away as gifts. Sometimes a friend asks me to build something new. This time it was a Celtic harp. I was building it out of California claro walnut, because I find the figure in the wood so fascinating, and because I love the way it smells when I work it—spicy and sweet. Different woods have different smells. Rosewood smells like—well, that's pretty obvious. Poplar smells like bacon as you saw and sand it. Cherry, I was sad to discover, doesn't smell like much of anything except hot wood.

Heidi Fluhr had joined me at the Montara house for the weekend. Heidi has her own aroma, and I find it intoxicating. If humans have pheromones, she's cornered the market. Heidi is an art dealer whose gallery is situated right under my Jefferson Street office near Hyde Pier, overlooking the Golden Gate. She specializes in post-modern art, but always carries a few traditional representational pieces, because they sell well with tourists looking for mementos of their trip to San Francisco. She's tall, blonde, and curvy, a Northern European goddess.

We met a few years back when she hired me for protection, after being robbed on the way to make a deposit. I tailed her for a few days, until the guy decided to take another swipe at her, whereupon I showed him what a bitch it is to exceed the limits of your Blue Cross coverage. She paid her bill immediately and added a tip by taking me out to dinner, which led to a night I shall carry fondly in my memory until the day I die.

We've been an item ever since. Maybe she's my girlfriend. I know she isn't anyone else's girlfriend. I'm not seeing anyone else, either, but that doesn't mean we see ourselves together for life. We get along, understand each other, and have a hell of a time between the sheets, but beyond that we avoid placing a label on what we do together, because that would imply permanence. We take it day by day and night by night. So far, it's worked out quite nicely. That's about as deeply as we've defined things.

On our previous sojourn to Montara, I'd laminated three boards of the claro walnut to make a slab about three inches thick, from which I would bandsaw the main upper arch of the harp. A Celtic harp is a lap instrument, not much larger than your typical moving box. I could make the entire arch with just one board of the walnut. After sawing out the basic shape, I'd attack it with rasps and files and assorted hand rifflers to carve out the delicate yet robust shape of the arch.

I lifted the slab onto my workbench and placed a heavy cardboard template over it. Using a pencil, I drew the outline of the main arch.

Heidi sat on the couch, wearing an oversized mesh Forty-Niners jersey, a serene smile, and that's about it. German by birth, she had grown up in a decidedly non-uptight environment when it came to body culture. She had on about as much as she ever did when we were at the beach. She was playing a Hauser replica classical guitar I had built several months earlier just for her, and she was doing it expertly.

I don't know a great deal about Heidi's youth. I know—entirely by chance—that her father was some high muckety in the German government. I know she doesn't go by the name she was given at birth. I know she is a trained classical musician who somehow found herself immersed in the Munich punk rock scene, and from there became involved in radical anarchist German politics, the kind that involve bombings and public mass shootings. I know she had to flee Germany under threat of death from her radical compatriots after she betrayed them in some way. I know she can never play guitar professionally in public again, because people who still want to hurt her might recognize her, and therefore the gallery is her way of staying in touch with her artistic side.

I could find out more, of course. It's kind of my thing. But Heidi asked me not to, and I've respected her wishes. We have that sort of relationship.

She played a piece I hadn't heard before on the Hauser knock-off. It was haunting and lyrical and would have driven Segovia himself to tears. Then, she stopped.

"Was that Brandon Hunt I saw head up to your office yesterday?" she asked, with a faint remnant of her German accent.

"Friend of yours?" I said as I stowed the template back in a rack.

"Hardly."

"But you know who he is."

"I watch the news. I read the paper. I know things. He's kind of famous."

"For all the wrong reasons."

"What did he want?" She rose from the sofa and placed the Hauser copy back on its wall hook.

"Got jumped a few days back on the university campus. Wants protection."

Heidi lounged on the sofa and picked up a novel she'd brought for the weekend. "I find the man reprehensible. He's a fascist."

"Something you Germans know a little about."

"And how."

"I don't think Brandon Hunt is looking to overthrow the government and install a totalitarian dictatorship," I said. "He just hates everyone who isn't him."

"He's a dick growing out of another smaller dick," she said.

The image was confounding. I turned to face her and cocked my head a little. She giggled, and I laughed out loud. I dusted myself off with a barber brush, tossed my shop apron on the workbench, and grabbed a couple of brews from the kitchen before joining her on the sofa.

"Are you taking the case?" she asked.

"Haven't decided. If I do, I might hand it over to Sonny Malehala."

"Is Sonny ready?"

"He's completely healed after getting shot to shit last year. He finished rehab a month ago. He's done a good job learning the data mining systems I use. I've already assigned him a couple of private security jobs, but that was just consulting. He's beginning to tug at the leash. He's restless. Wants some action."

"Do you think he'll see any, bodyguarding Brandon Hunt?"

"I think Hunt is just unpopular enough to merit a second pummeling. Maybe a third. If someone tries, Sonny can put a stop to it. Mostly, though, a half-Polynesian dude saving Hunt's bacon would drive him nuts. I like the mental image of him twisting in the wind, chewing at his tongue in frustration."

"You're kind of scary when you get devious." Heidi snuggled up to me.

"Ain't it da truth?" I said.

THREE

On Monday, I caught up with Sonny Malehala working out on a heavy bag at the 3rd Street Boxing Gym in the Dogpatch District near the Bay. He saw me walk in and waved me over.

"Bring your gloves? We could spar," he said.

"I'm not in the mood for major medical bills," I told him.

Sonny goes about six-five. In both directions. When I first met him, he was working security for an aging gangster named Junius Bugliosi, whom some people called JuneBug at their peril. He was perfectly suited to the job. His size and experience as an Army Ranger made him both scary and effectively violent. His looks were a bonus. Of Polynesian extraction, when he shaved his head, he looked remarkably like a popular action movie star, so much so that he occasionally had to fend off persistent autograph hunters. Lately, he'd let his hair grow to about a half inch, which lay flat against his skull and made him look dark and dangerous.

Which he is.

A few months back, Sonny almost died failing to protect Bugliosi from being assassinated. Shortly after, as he recuperated from bullet wounds that almost cost him use of his right arm, he took me up on an offer to teach him the private cop trade. I handed him the easy scut work during his rehab. Lately, fully recovered—and, if possible, bigger than when I first met him—he had expressed a desire to get his hands a little dirtier.

"Got a job for me?" Sonny hefted a plastic bottle and squirted a stream of energy drink into his mouth.

"Not sure yet. Have a possible new client. Every heard of Brandon Hunt?"

He glowered and raised one eyebrow, an expression that got him a lot of attention in public.

"The college professor?" he asked.

"The very same."

Sonny pulled off his gloves and took a seat at the bench press, after putting about a hundred pounds on each end of the bar.

"Light workout today?"

"Just warming up, my friend. Brandon Hunt, huh? Yeah, I know who he is. Hope you're here to tell me someone's put a contract on him."

"Almost. A gang of toughs used him as a hacky sack the other night."

"Would it be insensitive of me to hope he sustained uncomfortable injuries?" Sonny lay on his back and grasped the weight bar. "Spot me?"

I stood at the head of the bench and braced my legs. I had no idea what I might do if he lost control of the bar. Probably start looking for a new partner.

"He's banged up. He's scared," I said.

Sonny lifted the bar the way most people heft a broomstick, did five quick reps, and placed it back on the hooks.

"My heart bleeds," he said, barely breathing heavily. He added thirty pounds to the bar and returned to the bench. "What's he want?"

"Protection."

"Damn. Fresh out," he said, and did five more reps. Some of the other guys in the gym stopped what they were doing to watch him. I didn't blame them. It was kind of a spectacle. "Put on another couple of ten pounders for me?"

As I attached the weights on the bar, I tried another approach.

"You still owe me for your training."

"You know anyone bigger than me you can send to collect?" He hoisted the bar and did five more reps. Then he sat up. "Look, Eamon, I get it. The guy hacks you off. He hacks everyone off. That's his thing. He's like half the made guys I ever met—grown up bullies. I'll bet Hunt was the biggest kid in his fifth grade class. Early developer. Got a head start on the other kids. Pair that with a bad attitude and general misanthropy, and you got your ingredients for a major league bully. Then, in junior high, suddenly all the kids he used to bounce around shot past him in size, and he had to find a new way to intimidate people."

"You sound like you're familiar with the type."

"I was the kid who got bounced around in the fourth grade. By ninth grade, the kid who bullied me regretted it. Hunt is still a bully, only he intimidates by flinging his shitty opinions around as if they were gospel and demeaning anyone who disagrees with him. He's a fucking narcissist with racist and xenophobic overtones. Nothing will ever be his fault. He blames everything on someone else. Worst thing that ever happened to him was winning that lawsuit against the university. It emboldened him. Nothing more dangerous than an emboldened asshole. Add twenty."

I positioned the weights, and Sonny reclined on the bench. His sweaty arms and shoulders bulged ominously as he pressed the bar five times. He sat up again and drank a little more of the energy slop.

"Eamon, I owe you," he said. "I know it. You took me out of a pretty bad place. I was getting sucked down into the mob shit, and you threw me a lifeline. I'm grateful. I really am. I can see the truth in your eyes, though. Hunt pisses you off as much as he does me. Why are you thinking of taking this case, anyway? You're bucks up. You can afford to kick back until something juicy comes along."

"I don't know," I said. "Maybe it's because he's friends with Earleen Marley. I owe Earleen a few solids."

"Totally reasonable. Loyalty and friendship. But think about it for a second. Do you really think Hunt wants someone like *me* shadowing his ass around campus? He'll take one look at me and faint dead away. On second thought, I might take the job just for that. No, this one's for you. He'll trust you, if only because you share similar pigmentation. You need backup, though, you got my number in your phone."

"You know," I said. "You just gave me an idea."

FOUR

The *Chronicle* ran a report about the attack on Brandon Hunt the next day. Ordinarily, a street assault didn't carry enough weight for six inches of column space, but Hunt's inflammatory op-ed letters and tweets had made him something of a celebrity, so getting his ass whupped was news. According to the account, the case was being investigated by an SFPD gold shield named Dexter Spears.

I knew Spears. I'd indirectly caused his partner's death in a Chinatown tong war a couple of years back. It was still a painful memory since Spears' partner had also been *my* partner when I was on the job.

To make matters worse, Spears was an exemplary fuckup, a politically appointed nepotistic favor for some long-retired police chief. I think he bought his brains from a vending machine each morning. I wasn't surprised he snagged Brandon Hunt's case. The cops hated Hunt as much as everyone else, so it was natural they'd toss his assault case to the one inspector constitutionally incapable of solving it.

The empty suit sat across from me in his office at the SFPD main office, which—coincidentally—was only a few blocks from the 3rd Street Boxing Gym. Spears was tall and rangy, built like a human whippet, but with eyes straight out of a fish market display case. His suit hung lazily on his body as if even it didn't want to be too close to him.

"It's an open case," he said, after I told him why I was visiting.

"I know. That's why I'm here. I don't want to step on any toes."

"Good thing, too. We take a dim view of private cops interfering with criminal investigations."

"Not my purpose. Hunt wants to hire me to provide protection. I already told him I wasn't interested in finding the guys who bounced him around the other night. Except to take them out for a beer, maybe."

"Rubs you the wrong way, too?" Spears asked.

"Under normal circumstances, I wouldn't touch him with *your* hands. If I take the case, I'm doing it for a mutual friend."

"What about that hood you hired last year? Minnehaha? Is he in on this protection deal?"

"It's Malehala and you know it. Right now, he's ancillary."

Spears gave me the dead-eye gawp again.

"Not directly involved," I explained. "Are you gonna help me out or what?"

Spears settled back in his chair and scratched vigorously at his scalp. I reminded myself not to shake hands with him when I left. Finally, he sighed. "Whatever. He was attacked by the fieldhouse on the way to the parking garage. It was roughly nine-thirty."

"Why was he leaving campus so late?"

"He had an evening class. Meets one day a week. Runs from six to nine. So, after chatting with a couple of students, he set off to his car. He cut between the fieldhouse and Cox Stadium to save time."

"Did he do that often?" I asked.

"Beats me. People are creatures of habit. He probably does."

"The guys who beat him up. Did they rob him? Take anything?"

"No. It was straight assault and battery."

"Did he describe them?"

"They didn't talk much. It wasn't like they stopped him for a cigarette and then jacked him. He was jumped. The guys wore hoodies. He never saw their faces before they bagged him. You should have asked him all this stuff when he hired you."

"He hasn't hired me yet, and I did ask. I'm looking for inconsistencies." I tried not to roll my eyes as I said it.

"All he saw was some guys in hoodies. Might have been wearing masks, or maybe gaiters, because he doesn't remember anything about race or facial features, and like I said, they didn't say much. They put a bag over his head, kicked the shit out of him, and ran away."

"TV cameras?"

"It's a blind spot. We think they split up after they left. Several cameras caught individual guys in hoodies walking along the sidewalk a few minutes later, but no groups."

"Where did these individuals go?"

"We lost all of them. This is new information. We only finished analyzing the camera footage last night. Each of them walked into another blind spot and disappeared.

"Doesn't sound like gang shit to me," I said. "Sounds like pros. Hired muscle."

"How do you figure?"

"Presuming it wasn't some random beatdown, Hunt was targeted. Whoever attacked him knew where to do it without becoming famous. They also bet heavily that Hunt would wander into that blind kill zone, which means they'd cased him. If he only works late one night a week, they might have been planning it for a month or more. They were smart enough to separate after the fact, and to get scarce quick. Probably ditched the hoodies in trash cans while they were in blind spots. That suggests a plan."

"You think they were hired?"

"A few thousand people in this town would love to toss Hunt off a bridge, but I don't see five of them somehow joining up to jump him without doing any serious, permanent bodily injury. They bag him, kick him a few times, leave some cuts and bruises, but they don't break any bones or blind him or stab him. If they were gangbangers trying to make their bones, they'd have just shot him. They pulled their punches. These guys had a ton of self-restraint, which suggests they weren't emotionally involved."

"So who hired them?" Spears asked.

"Someone who wanted to send a message."

"What message?"

"That's the question, isn't it?" I said. "If you've been listening, Inspector, I just provided you with a lead."

"We'll follow up," he said. I noticed he didn't thank me. "You gonna take the protection gig?"

"I'm leaning toward it," I said. "I think Brandon Hunt may be in deeper trouble than we know. He may bear close watching."

"Well, stay out of our way, and we'll be jake."

FIVE

I met Sonny Malehala for lunch at Nob Hill Café, not far from his condo near Powell and California Streets. I ordered the eggplant parmigiana. Sonny went with the veal piccata. We both had a generous pour of the house table red.

"Who hires out muscle in the area?" I asked.

"Why? You thinking about taking a run at Brandon Hunt? Because, like, I'd be totally down, man."

"I think someone already did."

He did the eyebrow thing. "Really," he said. It wasn't a question.

"I talked with the police inspector on the case. His description dovetails with the account Hunt gave, and it all sounds like someone hired some thugs to do some speedbag drills on Hunt's face. They sound like pros. So, I figured maybe you might know some people who are still in the life."

"In the *life?*" Sonny said. "Eamon, we have been over this. I wasn't a hood. I worked security for Mr. Bugliosi. I stood around scowling and looking like I could shoot the nuts off a hamster at thirty yards—which I *can*, by the way—

and that's it. I carried a gun, sure, but I only pointed it at someone three times, and once was at *you*."

I remembered. "I think someone is sending Hunt a message."

"I think a lot of people are sending him messages."

"Maybe someone thought he needed to pay better attention. Hunt's scared, which sounds like a new emotion for him. Maybe he knows something that frightens him, but he hasn't told us about it yet. Are you still in? What we discussed last night?"

"Sure."

"Good. I think, after lunch, I'll head over to the university."

"You're taking the case, then?"

"I think so. I want to talk to Earleen Marley first."

"Earleen, huh?" His eyes lit up for the first time since I'd impugned his reputation.

"You interested?" I asked. "I hear she and her fiancé split a few months back."

"Yeah? Well, maybe you could feel her out…"

"What are we, eighth-graders? Call her yourself. You're both grownups. Hell, maybe she has a Tinder account. For a guy who can crush a Volkswagen like a beer can, you can be a real weenie sometimes."

"You really think she's on Tinder?" he asked.

"Jesus, Sonny. Call her."

"All right. Hey, if you take this gig with Hunt, we'll be hanging out at the university anyway. Might be a good opportunity to know her better."

———————

"My *kohai* Sonny totally wants to bounce your bones," I told Earleen as I plopped onto the sofa in her office. "But you didn't hear that from me."

Earleen was tall, athletic, and very attractive. She had let her hair go natural that year, and it suited her, as it highlighted her coffee complexion and chestnut eyes, even if it did increase her height to that of the average NBA point guard. Wouldn't be a problem for Sonny, though. Or for me, for that matter, but Heidi was all I could handle.

"Is that a fact?" she said.

"He asked me on the playground today to find out if you liked him. It was cute as shit."

"Your *kohai?* Does that make you the *sensei?*"

"*And for some men, greatness is bestowed upon them.*"

"Tell Sonny to give me a call."

"I did."

She nodded, and I could see an anticipatory twinkle in her eyes. I hadn't told Sonny that Earleen was San Francisco born and bred, to parents who used to groove to Jerry and the Dead back in the Haight-Ashbury days, and had extremely sex-positive attitudes. If she found you attractive, she was kind of a sure thing. I'm not telling tales out of school. We'd had this discussion before, shortly after we first met, when she came onto me. I'd demurred, citing my ongoing-but-otherwise-undefined monogamous situation with Heidi, but we'd spent a stimulating evening discussing the hypothetical possibilities. A couple of months ago, she started casually dropping Sonny's name in our conversations. The planets were aligning. I felt like a fucking *yenta.*

The matchmaking completed, she turned to business. "I suppose you're here to talk about Brandon."

"I am."

"Are you taking the case?"

"There's no case to take. The cops are investigating the attack. Hunt just wants a bodyguard. I've about decided to help him out. If I'm right, he might be in some danger, and I can make a lot of bank on that."

"So it's just about the money."

"Bucks before yucks," I said. "And don't use that Bene Gesserit psychotherapist voice on me. I'm immune. How is it you and Hunt are friends in the first place? You live in different universes."

"We have a sentimental attachment. I banged him a couple of times."

I cringed. "Jesus, Earleen. Now I gotta pour Clorox on my brain."

"It was years ago, just after he arrived on campus, before I realized he's a pig. It never would have worked. He was a selfish lover. We had a connection, though. Beats the hell out of me, too. Probably something chemical. Anyway, I can tolerate him in long stretches, which says something. Not many people can. I guess that's one measure of friendship."

"So he's always been a dickhead?"

"Not publicly. When you join the faculty at a university, you're essentially in kiss-ass mode until you earn tenure. You take whatever shitty committee spots your supervisor can't push off on anyone else. You teach eight sections of intro psych with a hundred fifty students in each class. You are absolutely not allowed to duck out on graduation, the single most boring three hours of every year. Your contract is year-to-year, so you don't rock the boat. Brandon wasn't as...um, *open* about his beliefs during his early years here. He didn't write long, xenophobic screeds for the local paper, or preach racial differences in his classroom."

"What about in private?" I asked.

"In private, he spouted some pretty radical shit. Word gets around. *Who's Afraid of Virginia Wolfe* was a documentary. A university faculty is a closed community. People talk. When it came time for Brandon to be evaluated for tenure, the review board was aware of his...distasteful opinions. After the lawsuit, when Brandon was reinstated, and the university was ordered to grant retroactive tenure— and to pay a hefty punitive award as well—Brandon blossomed. It was like he had been in the closet for a decade, and finally it was cool to come out. With tenure, he could say anything he wanted, and he did. And he still does."

"Sonny thinks the worst thing that ever happened to Hunt was winning the court case."

"Brandon would disagree. That was his Sweet Sixteen coming out party. Finally, he could be himself, with no restraints. He's certainly capitalized on it."

"What about the hypocrisy? The guy's an out-and-out racist, but...I mean...you and he..."

"Yep. It looks hypocritical. But remember, I didn't know who he was at the time. Between you and me, whenever we were in bed, I think Brandon fantasized about Thomas Jefferson and Sally Hemmings. I think a situation like that would be very arousing for him."

"And that didn't repel you?"

She shrugged. "Everyone has their own sexual scripts, Eamon. Everyone fantasizes, sometime."

I got the message. Earleen was a little turned on by the notion as well. Everybody's a little kinky. I've known women who fantasized about gangbangs but would be horrified if ever confronted with one. When it comes to sex, our heads are frequently screwed on sideways.

"Like I said, the real problem is he was a selfish lover. That's kind of a dealbreaker. We agreed to stay friends, so I didn't drop him just because he became a complete public jerk after the trial. Friends stick with each other, right? So, you're taking this on?"

"Yeah. But our slates are clean, now, right? We're even on favors?"

"Don't do this because of me," she said. "Remember what I said. You deal with Brandon, and you might get burned."

"I'll wear my Brooks Brothers firesuit," I said.

SIX

Brandon Hunt's office door was locked. The schedule taped to it said he was teaching a course in forensic psychology two buildings down and would be for the next forty-five minutes. I could have cooled my heels in the lounge down the hall, but I'd already decided to bill Hunt for the hours I'd put in, so he was on the meter. I decided to use the time constructively and see exactly who was hiring me.

The classroom was a tiered amphitheater, twenty rows deep, and packed with students. Not surprisingly, the classroom lights were dimmed, but a floodlight illuminated the lectern area like a motion picture set. Hunt liked to ensure that people could see him, and the dim classroom lights discouraged all that distracting note-taking. Not that the students took notes anymore. I glanced around and saw about fifty pocket digital recorders on my first pass. I took an empty seat on the back row and watched.

A projector threw a picture of a graph on a huge screen pulled down in front of the widest whiteboard I'd ever seen. The graph appeared to represent data from the FBI's National Incident Based Report system on geographic distribution of violent crime. Hunt stood at his lectern, his face still bandaged, and he highlighted key lines of the report with a red laser pointer.

"So, you see," he said, "When you analyze violent crimes—rape, assault, murder—you find a significantly higher frequency of these crimes in geographic areas with higher numbers of minorities. Geographic profiling can assist the police in focusing greater force in the areas where crime is happening, rather than wasting manpower on less dangerous areas such as the suburbs."

A young blonde woman in the front row raised her hand. Hunt looked irritated. He jabbed a finger at her.

"Yes?" he said, impatiently.

"Dr. Hunt, you seem to assert that the higher crime rates in inner cities are directly attributable to the higher proportions of minorities in those areas."

"Not only minorities, but also immigrants, many of them illegal. Why do you ask?"

"Is that the only possible explanation?"

Hunt placed the laser pointer on the lectern and faced the girl. "You seem to want to make a point."

"Is it possible that there are other factors you haven't cited that also explain the higher crime rates?"

"Like what?" Hunt asked.

"Population density, to begin with. Dr. Calhoun's behavioral sink theory…"

"Child," Hunt said, sneering. "Dr. Calhoun's study was sixty years ago." He turned to the rest of the class. "Everyone know the study Suzie Q. here is citing? No?" He turned back to the girl. "There's a reason. It's…ancient…history. For the benefit of the class, however…"

Hunt turned off the projector, grabbed a dry-erase marker and raised the screen. He drew a large circle on the board and a much smaller circle in the center of it.

"John B. Calhoun experimented on rats. He placed one rat in an enclosure." Hunt pointed to the small circle in the center of the larger circle. "He measured the frequency and magnitude of antisocial or degenerate behavior—which, for rats, mostly means fighting, biting, and screwing. Territorial behaviors. Not surprisingly, a single rat was boring. When he put two dozen or so rats in the same enclosure, however, aggressive territorial behaviors emerged. Rats fought over food, even though there was plenty for everyone. Boy rats copulated with other boy rats. Rats murdered each other for no apparent reason. It looked a lot like downtown Oakland on a Saturday night."

A few titters rose from the audience. Hunt held for the laugh and continued.

"Calhoun, in his analysis, suggested that it was the population density itself that caused the behaviors, because that was the only factor he manipulated. That was the entire scope of his hypothesis. He didn't measure for anything else. So, now, Miss Nebraska here in the front row asserts that, based on Calhoun's research, the real source of violent criminal activity in inner cities is population density. Does that sum it up, dear?"

The girl looked around her, suddenly realizing Hunt was ridiculing her in front of the class. "That...that's right," she said.

"Calhoun conducted his research in 1960. Way before the civil rights movement gained steam. Back then, races were segregated. Minorities knew their place."

"Oh, fuck this shit!" a young black man said. He stood, walked up the aisle and out the door, slamming it as he exited. I heard him huffing angrily as he passed me. Hunt seemed delighted.

"Another county heard from," he exulted. "Don't worry. Mr. Richardson hasn't left us permanently. He needs this class to keep his sports scholarship, which is the only way he was ever going to get into college. Now, as I was saying, Calhoun performed his experiment long before the civil rights movement convinced minorities to try to rise above their station. He conducted it when women were still bound to the home by their menstrual cycles, the way God intended, before the pill came along. He conducted it, in scientific terms, in the distant past. He might as well have run his little rat farm during the English Reformation. It would be as relevant. The world today is different. All the traditional values on which this country was built have been tossed out the window. None of the old rules apply. Crime in the black community skyrocketed after the Civil Rights Act of 1964 was enacted—four years after Calhoun conducted his study. He didn't look at race because crime within the black community was no higher, overall, than among the white community, prior to 1964. For Calhoun, the problem didn't exist yet. Now, having established that crime in the black community has risen geometrically since 1964, and given that we know inner cities are more densely populated than suburban areas, and that those populations are more densely populated by minorities, we have a new explanation for higher frequency of inner city crime. That's where the *criminals* live."

Hunt hovered over the girl who'd asked the question.

"But, if you want to go down Calhoun's rabbit hole, you're perfectly free to do so. And I assure your grade will reflect your detour. Any other questions?"

The girl had her back to me, but I could see her swipe at her cheek with her fingers.

"No," she said, softly.

Hunt returned to his lectern. He started to turn the projector back on. Instead, he placed both hands on the lectern and looked over the hundred or so students in the lecture hall.

"Science," he started, "is and must be *objective*. When confronted with data that suggests ugliness in our society, we cannot simply ignore that data because it makes us uncomfortable. The problem with most liberal researchers is that they reject ugly explanations for social phenomena. They filter their findings through their rose-colored glasses. They genuinely believe that all people are created good, and when someone behaves badly it must be because society has somehow failed them. Well, boo-fucking-hoo. Let me tell you something, children. Evil exists. Some people are born bad. We call them psychopaths. And the data on criminal convictions strongly suggests a racial disparity in the distribution of psychopaths. The prison population in this country is fifty-nine percent black and Hispanic, whereas those populations account for only thirty-one percent of the population at large. Again, a racial disparity. It may pain us as a society to admit it, but we have a race problem here, and we did it to ourselves by breaking with centuries of societal tradition in a very short period of historic time. We ran before we were ready to walk."

He stopped and surveyed the rows of students, and he sighed. "But I can see in your faces that I'm wasting my time. Class fucking dismissed."

SEVEN

I remained seated as the students filed out and Hunt gathered his things.

"Weren't you a little rough on her?" I asked when he and I were alone. Hunt jerked his head up.

"Who is that?" he demanded. He flipped a wall switch, and the auditorium lights came up. "Gold? Is that you?"

He yanked a pair of glasses from his pocket and slipped them on, peering up at me.

"There are other factors, you know," I said.

"Factors? Factors for what?"

"The higher percentage of minorities in prison compared to the general population."

"Yeah? Like what?"

I stood. "Police target minorities and let whites off the hook. Prejudiced judges give disparate sentences, shuffling minorities off to prison but giving whites probation. Private prisons force states into contractual obligations to incarcerate as many people as possible and keep them locked up. A general tendency in cops to report feeling more 'threatened' by minorities during routine traffic stops. There are more."

"All excellent arguments, and valid ones. Miss Nebraska never cited any of them. You know why?"

I waited.

"Because she's vapid," he said. "She has the brain of one of Calhoun's rats. She belongs back in Omaha, working in a Dairy Queen and squeezing out babies with different last names. Three days ago, she sat in my office and offered to blow me for a passing grade. I told her Linda fucking Lovelace couldn't save her ass unless she really hit the books and learned a thing or two. Today was her trying to look smart and failing. I do wish she had made all the same arguments you did, Gold. If she had, there might be hope for her. What do you want?"

"I've decided to take you on as a client."

He hoisted his battered leather briefcase by its strap and slipped it onto his shoulder. "What sold you?"

"I talked to the SFPD inspector handling the case. I don't think your attack was random."

"Of course it wasn't. If you haven't heard yet, Gold, I'm not a popular guy. People don't like being told hard truths. They push back against them. You should see some of the Twitter responses I get, and the emails."

"I want to," I said. "And you should share them with Inspector Spears as well. They're potential evidence. Let's take a walk and discuss the scope of what I can provide."

"Did you walk directly from your class to the parking lot on the night you were assaulted?" I asked as we exited through the automatic doors of Hunt's classroom building.

"Yes," he replied.

"Let's reenact it. I want you to take the same route you took that night."

He pointed toward Cox Stadium and the fieldhouse. "I took a shortcut that night, because I was in a hurry to get home."

"Why?"

"It's not important. Not relevant."

"Everything's relevant when you don't know anything, and we're starting from scratch here."

We passed Sonny Malehala, who sat on a bench reading a novel. He wore an SFSU sweatshirt and jeans. Sonny and I didn't make eye contact, per our plan. I'd decided, since we were probably dealing with hired muscle, that it wouldn't hurt to have a spare pair of eyes on Hunt.

See, the movies get it all wrong. Sonny and I, *mano a mano*, can take care of ourselves. Put either of us up against a gang of thugs, and we'd probably wind up looking just like Hunt. Maybe worse, because we'd fight back. A private detective in the movies takes on five kung-fu ninjas and walks away from the unconscious bodies with barely mussed hair. In real life, go up against more than a couple of average hoods, and you're in for an ass-kicking. Face off against five pros, and you might move into an urn.

If I was right, someone wanted to send Hunt a message, but didn't want him dead. I'm kind of hard to miss, escorting

Hunt around campus. Sonny just looked like an admittedly senior fullback cramming for a lit exam. If the black flag was hoisted, though, I had backup, and Sonny had the element of surprise. He could also surreptitiously keep an eye on Hunt when I was otherwise occupied. This way, Sonny also didn't have to interact with Hunt, which suited him, and he had my six, which suited me.

"You don't like me much, do you, Gold?" Hunt asked as we neared the stadium.

"Does it matter?" I asked.

"I would like to think you're in this for more than just a paycheck. I'd like to think you took the job because you cared for my wellbeing."

"Sure. I want you to stay good and healthy. I hate squeezing money out of estate executors."

"Have you ever lost a client?"

"It's happened. I wouldn't worry about it, though. They were just practice. I have better game now." I kept my eyes straight ahead, and struggled to keep my face stolid, because I could see him gawp at me in peripheral vision. I pointed toward the stadium. "I played there, you know."

"I didn't know."

"I was a student here in different century. Football scholarship."

"Weren't good enough for the pros, huh?" he asked.

"We'll never know. I blew out my knee my junior year. Kept me out of the pro draft, but not off the force. That kid who blew up in your class today?"

"Richardson," he said.

"You know his story?"

"He's a jock. What is there to know?"

"Your class—forensic psychology? I suppose there's only one section a semester."

"Only one a year. I alternate with developmental psych."

"How many students take intro psych here?"

"Almost all of them. It's one of the most popular general education courses. Why do you ask?"

"Part of being a detective is asking questions. I see a pretty woman or a well-dressed man sitting alone at a restaurant table, and I wonder *why*. Have they been stood up? Are they introverts? Is it a first date, and one person arrived early? What will happen when the other person shows up? Or doesn't? Lots of questions. I guess I'm just the curious and imaginative type. You have an upper level course that meets once a year and has a student cap of—what?—a hundred students?"

"Eighty. Why?"

"So, almost every student here takes intro, but only eighty get your forensic course each year. I'm imagining a scholarship athlete, standing around the gym during registration—"

"We don't do that anymore. Registration is online now."

"—Sitting at his computer during registration, then. He's trying to figure out what to take. A stereotypical jock might look for a crip course. Richardson, though, chose one of the most exclusive—and I'd imagine difficult—courses on campus."

"It is extremely popular. Fills up in minutes each year."

"Well, I'm sure you'd admit that a fair share of them are taking the course for the same reason they visit carnival freak shows, right?"

"What do you mean?"

"You're something of a celebrity. An *enfant terrible.*"

"French. I'm impressed."

"You should see me order a crepe. Some of your students just come to watch you pop off at whatever social group is in your craw that week. And I bet you're a tough grader."

"Everyone gets the same treatment, Gold."

"No doubt. So, since I'm in the question asking business, I have to ask why a kid like Richardson would take your course in the first place. He has to know you have a hard-on for minorities. If he has any hope of making the pros, his scholarship is sacred. If he's just a dumb jock, why take a chance of dinging his grade point average with your course?"

"Did you come up with an answer?"

"When the kid stormed out of the classroom, you humiliated him publicly, claiming that he was only in college to play ball, and probably wouldn't have been admitted otherwise."

"So?"

"Maybe it's not an either-or situation. Maybe he's a jock *and* a serious student."

"I love that Boy Scout head of yours, Gold. Your balloon never lands, does it?"

"*I* was a jock *and* a serious student. You chastised me the other day for playing dumb. When I told you I was here on a football scholarship, you hardly blinked."

41

"I can see you were big enough to be a jock."

"But you couldn't see that Richardson might be serious about getting an education?"

"What are you suggesting?"

"Just asking questions. Seems to me, though, you might want to get your vision checked. So, the other night, did you pass in front of or behind the fieldhouse?"

He pointed toward the front of the fieldhouse, to a narrow strip of land separating it from a utilities plant. "This way."

"Okay. We'll take the same route today. Tell me when we get to the place where you first saw the guys who beat you up."

He stopped near the center of the fieldhouse. "It was about here. It was night, of course, so we only had the overhead floodlights on. There were a lot of shadows. As I got to this spot, I saw the first of them come around the corner."

"Toward you?"

"Yes."

"What did he look like?"

Hunt closed his eyes. "Slightly taller than me. He wore a hoodie. His face was entirely in shadow. He might have been wearing sunglasses."

"At night?"

"So I couldn't see his eyes, maybe. To tell you the truth, I didn't pay him that much attention. Hoodies and jeans are pretty much the student uniform. As far as I was concerned, he was just on his way to the dorms across campus. That's when someone tossed a bag over my head, and people started punching on me. I thought there were three or four. The campus police video found five people wearing hoodies walking away from here in different directions afterward."

"Do you take this route to the garage frequently?"

"Once in a while, if I'm in a hurry."

"And you were in a hurry the other night."

"Yes," he said.

"But you can't say why."

"I choose not to. As I said, it's not relevant."

I told him to stay where he was, and I walked around the fieldhouse. I found five or six hidey-holes where someone could lie in wait. I could see how Hunt's story could have gone exactly as he described it.

I returned to the front of the fieldhouse, were Hunt waited.

"Okay," I said. "Here's what I think happened. As I told you, this wasn't a random jump. I believe these guys were hired to work you over."

"Oh, come on," Hunt said. "That's absurd."

"No. No it isn't. In fact, it makes the most sense. Nothing else fits. My next question is—"

"*Who?*" Hunt said. "I'm not entirely unfamiliar with asking questions myself, Gold."

"Okay," I said. "Who?"

"I haven't a clue."

"This wasn't intended to seriously injure you. You were supposed to recognize that. Someone either wants you to do something, or doesn't want you to do something, or you are in some profound debt to someone, and they want to collect. That kind of covers the waterfront. Who might fit in one of those categories?"

Hunt cocked his head, stared at me, and then turned and walked off a few yards. He placed his hands on his hips and bent over, gazing at the turf, as if undergoing an internal deliberation. Finally, he straightened, and walked back to me.

"What if I told you I was being blackmailed?" he asked.

EIGHT

Hunt's office was straight out of Academic Decorating magazine, classic edition. Books stacked everywhere. Hundreds of books. George Lincoln Rockwell. Nelson Rockefeller. Winston Churchill. A copy of Abbie Hoffman's *Steal This Book*. Textbooks galore, some with the spine peeling away. The place smelled of must and mildew and twenty years of butt sweat. He had the messiest desk I'd ever seen. Books, old candy wrappers, an open can of Coke, about a dozen pens strewn about, stacks of legal pads covered with scribbles, two open packs of gum, and a dog-eared copy of *Atlas Shrugged*.

To tell the truth, it looked staged.

I glanced outside. Sonny had relocated to a bench under Hunt's office window. With Hunt's back to me, I shot him with my finger. He shot back. It was sort of an improvised high sign.

Hunt rustled through his desk before pulling out a manila envelope. He passed it to me. "It's not the original," he said. "A copy."

It was a crude extortion letter. Attached to it was a digital photo, in which Hunt was clearly identifiable. The girl trying to give him artificial respiration from the entirely wrong end was more difficult to identify. The other girl, lying next to them on the bed, was displayed in crystal clarity. She was Asian. Purple hair. Maybe a wig. Looked to be in her twenties, but perhaps younger. Her blasted eyes and distended pupils and the weird grin on her face told me she'd altered her body chemistry. Cocaine or speed. Maybe mollies. With all the designer drugs out these days, it's easy to lose track.

"Photoshopped?" I asked.

"Ah...no," he said. "It happened. It's real."

"Shame on you, Professor. Mongrelizing around like this. One might suggest hypocrisy."

"I never said minorities don't have their place," he said, almost reflexively.

I narrowed my eyes and hovered over him. "Do you know the meaning of the word *defenestration?*"

He sat in his chair. "You don't have to threaten. I'm the one being blackmailed, you know. I'm the one who got beat up."

I pointed to the picture.

"Who are they? They look young."

"Sandy is," he said, indicating the Asian girl.

"Sandy?"

"Her real name is Tsuyako. Tsuyako Dennis."

"Sandy Dennis?" I said. "Really?"

"A dumb coincidence. Her parents adopted her when she was a baby. They're too young to remember the actress."

"So, who is she?" I asked.

"A co-ed. Psych major. Wants to go to grad school."

"And you're tutoring her in the finer points of the subject? Who's the other one? The blonde?"

"Beats me. A Tinder date. Sandy arranged it. I don't remember her name."

I scrutinized the picture again. "Who took the photo?"

"Sandy. With her cell phone."

"She's blackmailing you?"

He rubbed his face. "No. I already talked to her. First person I thought about when this showed up. She denied it completely. Was genuinely horrified. Someone hacked her phone and stole all her pictures—including with people other than me. Sandy's smart, but she's kind of a slut."

"You said this is a copy. Where's the original?"

"At home. Sealed in a plastic bag. As soon as I realized what it was, I secured it."

"Why?"

"Besides being a psychologist, I'm a criminologist. I know the value of preserving evidence."

"How'd you get it?"

"It came through campus mail."

I looked up. "Really?"

"It's ingenious when you think about it. The absolute lowest-tech way to deliver it. Completely untraceable."

"How do you mean?"

He pulled a large manila envelope from his desk. It was designed to close with a bit of string that wrapped around a button glued to the paper. On both sides of the envelope were rows of scored lines. Half of the front was already filled in with the names of other faculty members, followed by their building and office number. The last name was Hunt.

"There are thousands of these scattered all over campus," he said. "In every mailroom, every office, every faculty lounge. When a faculty member wants to send something to another faculty member, they just grab the nearest envelope, address it, stuff it, and toss it in the nearest campus mail bin."

"The last name before yours," I said. "Shirley Quattlebaum."

"A business professor. Her office is halfway across campus."

"Not a suspect?"

"We've never met, have no academic interests or committees in common. She'd have no reason to send me anything. Besides, that's not how it works. If I kept every envelope that comes to my office, I'd be inundated in no time. Every couple of days, I take all the accumulated campus mail envelopes down to the mail room and dump them in a collection bin. Everyone does. They get redistributed from there."

I thought it over. "So, anyone could just wander into a lounge or mailroom anywhere on campus and pick up one of these?"

"Yep."

"I see what you mean. Untraceable."

I read over the blackmail note once again. It was terse and direct.

You have two options. Take the honorable way out and resign or be terminated for moral turpitude. Resign or these pictures will be sent to the college president.

"When did you get this?" I asked.

"Four days before I was attacked."

"You can be fired for this?" I said. "Looks like private behavior to me."

"Sandy's a student," he said. "The other one might be as well. Things have changed. Back when I was a college student, taking a new co-ed for a lover each year was considered part of a professor's benefits package. Now? Unethical, indecent, and exploitative. And, a violation of university policy, even for professors with tenure. Boy, do I miss the good old days."

I leaned against the wall and folded my arms. "Blackmail is a felony. You should go to the police."

"I can't! The police hate me. If they even get a glimpse of this picture, it'll be on the front page of the *Chronicle* the next day."

"You think the extortion and your attack are related?"

"Don't you?" he argued.

"It doesn't track," I said. "Why beat you up? When you didn't quit, why didn't they just distribute the pictures?"

"I don't know!" he shouted. "That's why I hired you!"

"You hired me for protection. This is something else."

"Look, Gold, I need this to go away. Calling the police isn't an option. I might as well shoot myself here and save a quarter. I didn't tell you about the blackmail the other day because you weren't working for me yet. Now that you are…" He shrugged. "I need you to find out who sent this picture, and make sure they don't distribute it."

"How do you suggest I do that?" I said.

"You're big. You look tough and scary. Between you and that steroid junkie sitting on the bench outside, I bet you can intimidate it out of them."

"You made him?" I said, surprised.

"Please. I live on this campus. And, believe it or not, I'm a sports fan. I know every jock here. He stands out like a clown at a funeral. He's over forty, and you completely ignored him as we walked by. Not even curious. Either you're really lousy at what you do, or you're partners. Are you going to do this, or what?"

I thought it over. "You absolutely refuse to go to the cops?"

"Not an option," he said.

"Then I'll need the original blackmail letter and picture. Maybe I can find something in them that will give me some idea who sent it."

NINE

"He made Sonny?" Heidi said, her eyes wide. She nearly snorted wine from her nose.

"We shall not speak of this again," Sonny grumbled.

"The hell we won't!" Heidi said. "I almost peed myself."

We were out for Italian at Sodini's on Green Street in North Beach, not far from my Russian Hill condo. I had linguini with clams. Sonny went with lasagna. Heidi, never shy at the dinner table, had ordered most of the appetizer menu. How she gorged and still maintained her decidedly curvy, yet athletic physique mystified me. We had just uncorked our second bottle of house red and were getting a little loose.

"Excuse me," Heidi said. She stood and turned toward the back of the restaurant. "Have to winky-tink."

She glided toward the ladies', floating on a fermentation cloud. Sonny quickly turned serious.

"How'd he do it?" he asked.

"I gotta hand it to him. The guy's smarter than the average bear. Turns out brains are kind of a prerequisite to be a college professor. Besides, he's a little paranoid, being blackmailed and all. He's probably seeing thugs around every corner. Don't worry about it. You aren't a real private eye until you've been made. It's happened to me dozens of times."

"What's the story on the picture?"

I'd picked up the original from Hunt's apartment before returning to my condo. Hunt had sealed it and the blackmail note in a zipped plastic bag to prevent contamination. It was exactly what I would have done, though I'd be shocked if an examination found any prints other than Hunt's. Even an amateur knows not to leave hard evidence in a shakedown letter.

"The Asian girl, Sandy, met Hunt at a bar just off campus. It wasn't planned. He was killing time, just popping back a couple of beers and watching a Warriors game on the big screen. Sandy was with some friends. She'd taken one of Hunt's courses, and they struck up a conversation. Somewhere along the way, Sandy mentioned she had some molly back in her apartment. One thing led to another, yada yada yada. Next thing he knows, he's tripping balls and Sandy suggests they bring some fresh blood into the game. She pulls out her phone and thumbs through several profiles on Tinder with Hunt looking over her shoulder. Half an hour later, anonymous Blondie arrives, and the party shifts up into the heavy metal rock and roll. Sandy takes some pictures, her phone is hacked, and we get to enjoy this intensely satisfying dinner on Hunt's nickel because we're discussing the case."

"You suspect the blonde?"

"It's possible. The tryst was several months ago. If Blondie stole the pictures that night, I suppose she could have sat on them. I checked Tinder before dinner. Couldn't find her."

"No blondes?"

"Plenty of blondes," I said. "This is California, after all. The picture doesn't show her at her best angle. It's hard to find a match."

"So you talk with Sandy next," he said.

"Not yet. I have a better idea. The blackmail note was created on a laser printer. Not a bad idea, at first glance. Every typewriter has its own idiosyncrasies—chips on the striker, stuff like that—that makes it unique. Laser printers, not so much."

"At first glance," Sonny said.

"At first glance. Eamon Gold Detective Handbook Tip Number Twelve: Not many people know that every laser printer embeds identifying information on the printed sheet in the form of Machine Identification Code."

"How?"

"Little, strategically placed, light yellow dots. Each machine is unique. The dots record the serial number and other identifying information about the machine on each page."

"You can read this?" Sonny asked, before shoveling a trowel-sized bite of lasagna into his maw.

"No. But I know someone who can."

"So, what do you do with the serial number?"

"It's a clue," I said, as I twirled linguine around my fork. "We take it and do that detective stuff I taught you. We follow the trail as far as it takes us. Maybe it takes us all the way. Even if it doesn't, wherever we wind up is probably better than where we started."

Heidi exited the restroom and returned to the table. I freshened her wine. She chugged about half of it and set it back on the table. Her eyes were glassy.

"Want to go dancing?" she asked. "I want to go dancing."

"What do you think?" I asked Sonny.

"I think you're going dancing," he said.

"Want to come with?" I asked.

"Naw. I'm going home to brush up on being invisible. I seem to have lost the knack."

"Good thing," I said. "I told Hunt you'd be around tomorrow. I need you to keep an eye on him while I follow up on this laser printer angle."

He gave me a look that could stop a train. Major eyebrow stuff.

"Relax," I said. "You don't have to shadow him. You don't even have to speak to him. You're a security blanket. Your job is to stay in the vicinity and make sure he doesn't lose his shit because he thinks we've abandoned him. I'll return and nursemaid him as soon as I can."

TEN

I met with Barbara Ledford the next day. Barbara is a physics professor at Berkeley, specializing in optics, a field for which she was almost uniquely qualified. Unlike most of us, Barbara possesses a genetic mutation that allows her to see millions of discrete colors. She can tell the difference in light frequencies as small as one thousandth of a nanometer. She can see more colors than Sherwin Williams and Dutch Boy combined.

She's also an expert in computer imaging, some of which she pioneered personally. A while back, I brought her a photocopied yearbook photo of a twelve-year-old child who had grown into a seventy-year-old person of interest. She not only clarified the picture, but—with the help of another, much younger researcher—age-progressed it so perfectly that I knew immediately where to find my suspect. She claimed the work she had done with her partner on my job opened the door to a bright future filled with investors clutching fistfuls of cash. She intended, as she put it, to corner the milk carton market.

She was a petite and button-nosed ball of fire, with dark bobbed hair and blue eyes that missed nothing in her field of view, and was not at all unattractive for a woman nearing fifty. Her research partner, a kid in his twenties, agreed. They had embarked on a torrid affair shortly after making their synergistic discovery.

"Still banging your boy toy?" I asked as I took a seat in her office.

She held up her left hand. The reflection off the rock on her finger nearly blinded me.

"Go on," I said. "Really?"

"The boy is smitten," she said. "And I am totally grooving on all the office gossip."

"Congratulations?" I said.

"Hell, Eamon. I'm not going to *marry* him. Cubic zirconium. We're having fun with everyone. After a few months, we'll quietly call it off. For now, though, we're having a blast."

"Worldly experience meets youthful enthusiasm."

"And how. Speaking of which, still with Xena the Scandinavian Warrior Princess?"

"She's German, and yes."

"Looks Swedish to me," Barbara said. "What's up? Are you working a case, or did you just miss me? Oh! Wait!"

It appeared she had missed her morning dose of Adderall and had doubled up on caffeine. She opened a desk drawer and pulled out an envelope, which she slid across the desktop to me. I opened it. A check. Several zeroes.

"What's this?" I asked.

"Your cut. If it hadn't been for you, Rusty and I probably never would have discovered that our separate research programs were so compatible. We incorporated, destroyed most of our data, recreated it under our own roof, and sold it."

"Not exactly ethical," I said.

"Moonlighting is a hallowed academic tradition. If they don't like it, they should pay us more. So, what's up?"

"I'm working a case. My client's being blackmailed. The note he received was laser-printed."

"Fucking amateurs," she said. "Got it on you?"

I handed her the folder Hunt had given me. She glanced at the printout.

"Juicy," she said. "Hope it's someone I hate. You're in luck. I can see the Machine Identification Code dots."

"I couldn't see anything."

She pointed toward her face. "X-Men eyes. I suppose you want to know the printer manufacturer, model, and serial number."

"You read my mind."

"Piece of cake. Cool your heels. Be right back."

She hustled out of the office, leaving me to lounge and gather my thoughts. If I was lucky, the serial code on the printer would lead me directly to the person who wrote the note. I would be surprised if it were that easy, though. Things seldom are. I had a feeling I'd have to pay Sandy Dennis a visit, and there was always the matter of the mysterious blonde in the blackmail picture. Sandy could probably point me in her direction. She found the blonde in her Tinder app once. She could probably find her again.

Barbara returned and slapped a printout on the desk. "You're looking for a Hewlett-Packard Color LaserJet Model

3800," she said. "Serial number's on there too. Oh, and you are totally fucked."

"Oh good. Familiar surroundings," I said as I slid the note and Barbara's printout into the folder.

She pointed to the printer next to her desk. "HP Color Laserjet 3800. University of California system has a contract with HP to supply printers. A lot of businesses do as well. It's a workhorse. They're everywhere."

"Is that so?" I said.

"Might take you a while to track this puppy down."

"Or maybe it won't," I said. "I like to keep my glass half-full."

"Speaking of which, you and Heidi should get together with Rusty and me for dinner. Alice Waters is a friend of mine. I can get us into Chez Panisse."

"Sounds great," I said. "Maybe when I'm done with this case."

"Don't suppose you have the blackmail photo in that folder?"

"Why?"

"Might be identifying information encoded in it."

"I know where it came from, and who took it. Her phone was hacked."

"Oh well," Barbara said. "Probably couldn't have told much from a printout anyway. I was just indulging my prurient interest."

It was one of those days when it was advantageous to know a tech billionaire in Silicon Valley.

From Berkeley, I drove to Palo Alto, and the office of Aubrey Innes. Aubrey had a small electronics company that paid him a huge wad of cash every year. I'd plugged a hole in his supply chain, putting a couple of really stupid guys in jail for a few years. Ever since, he felt compelled to send me more business. Some of it was boring. Some of it had nearly killed me.

Aubrey is tall and lanky with thinning blonde hair edging over toward gray, and stylish eyeglasses. I had never seen him wear a tie. He offered me a drink as we shook hands. It sounded like a good idea.

"I'm working for a particularly obnoxious client," I said. "Normally, I'd like to pile on as many billable hours as possible, but in his case, I'm looking for shortcuts."

"How can I help?" he said.

"My client's being blackmailed. He received a laser-printed extortion letter. The MIC identified the machine."

I slipped the printout Barbara had given me across to him. He looked it over.

"A lot of these out there," he said.

"So I hear. I hoped you might know someone over at HP, and maybe that someone knows if there is a database somewhere detailing the purchaser of each serial numbered machine."

Aubrey glanced at the printout again. "Sure," he said. "No problem." He pulled out his cellphone and punched a number in his directory. "Hi, Bob! How's it going?"

After a minute or two of chitchat, he got to the point. We were in luck. Bob, whoever he was, said he'd call us back in few. While we waited, Aubrey and I passed the time.

"You heard about Jack?" he asked, referring to a construction and oil CEO he'd referred to me. "What a shame. To disappear in a plane crash like that."

"Yeah. I heard. Tough break." I also knew the true story, but I couldn't share it with Aubrey. Instead, we clinked glasses and toasted to his fallen buddy. I am, above all, a discreet investigator. Says so on my business cards.

Aubrey's cellphone rattled, and he answered it. He punched out within seconds.

"San Francisco State University," he said.

"What about it?"

"The printer was part of a bulk purchase by the university. Only a year ago, so it's probably still in service."

"They didn't know which department?"

"It doesn't work that way. The school orders 'em, and HP ships 'em on pallets in a big truck. It's up to the university where they wind up."

"But someone at the university should know," I said.

"Oh, yeah. Colleges are nuts about inventory. They keep better records than the IRS. They know where every computer, desk, chair, filing cabinet, printer, and coat rack is located. They check it every year—sometimes twice a year— to make sure nothing's walked off."

"Because stuff does," I said.
"You bet it does."

ELEVEN

I found Sonny soaking up some rays on the bench outside Hunt's office.

"Anything?" I asked.

"*Nada.* How about you?"

"The extortion note was produced on a laser printer which—at this moment—resides somewhere on this campus."

"Ah," he said. "Progress. You think it's a student?"

"Beats me. Half the faculty at this college hate Hunt. The campus cops would love to stuff him into a trash compacter. Maybe it was one of them. With the phone hacking, though, this smacks of something more sophisticated. The kind of thing a kid could do."

"They are savvy little buggers these days. Got bored sitting on benches, so I crashed Hunt's class this morning."

"Learn anything?" I asked.

"Mostly that our client is an asshole. You should charge him double for aggravation."

"What was today's subject?"

"As best I could tell, how the man of color is the white man's burden."

"He's kind of a broken record."

"Wrong thing got broke." Sonny took off his sunglasses and peered at me. "Are we doing the right thing protecting this dickweed, Eamon?"

"How do you mean?"

"I don't feel like I'm on the side of the angels on this one. Remember, I spent the last ten years working for people whose souls were mostly bile. All it got me was shot up."

"And a sweet condo in the ritziest zip code on the Bay."

"That was the carrot. You should have seen the stick," Sonny said. "I'm not naïve. I knew we weren't going to be working for nuns and social workers. This guy, though. Listening to him makes me curious whether screams carry through six feet of dirt."

"With any luck, he'll be a closed case in a few days. If we run this extortionist to ground, the heat will be off. After that, he's on his own. Take a hike. Go work out or get a massage or something. Forget about Hunt for the rest of the day. I'll take it from here."

Hunt took off early that afternoon, around four. I escorted him home, where he told me he expected to remain for the night, so I headed for the barn.

I took an hour or two to wrangle the pile of correspondence and billing that had accumulated on my desk. Then I loped down the stairs to Heidi's gallery. She had recently acquired a consignment from an up-and-coming abstract impressionist, which had generated a fair amount of floor traffic and disappointingly few sales. She closes at six, and by the time I arrived she was feeling kind of grumpy as she set the alarm.

"Good day?" she asked as she took my arm and we strolled toward Pier 39.

"Fair to middlin'," I said. "Made some progress. Nobody buying today?"

"Mostly looky-loos. I sold one piece, and not a very expensive one. Only three thousand. Fucking recession is killing me."

"Would a nice Dungeness crab salve your wounds?"

"Is he an art collector?"

We headed for a place on the pier where they knew us by name. We were seated immediately, despite the line outside, and settled into our booth under the glare of disapproving tourists. I ignored them. When I come to their town, they can take first seating.

We ordered a couple of crabs, a salad, and a bottle of Riesling. While we waited, I told her what I could about my day's exploits. She was particularly interested in the goings-on between Barbara Ledford and Rusty.

"She's a quarter century older than him," she said. "What in hell do they have to talk about?"

"From what I understand, there isn't much talking. Though, they do have their shared work. I think it's much more a physical thing. Besides, there's a sizeable gap in our ages, and we get by."

"It's not, like, twenty-five years!"

"No, and for that I'm grateful. You'd probably put me in a hospital."

"But then I could nurse you. Do you expect to locate the printer tomorrow?"

"With luck. I want to talk to this young woman in the blackmail photo first, though. Something about Hunt's story doesn't sit right."

"What's bothering you?"

"It just doesn't track. He received the extortion note and squirreled it away. Several days later, someone kicked the tar out of him. I don't see the connection. Blackmailers don't send legbreakers. They just release whatever embarrassing shit they have if you don't pay up, make an example out of you, and move on to the next mark. I think the two things may not be related at all."

"And if they aren't?"

"Then Doctor Hunt may be in deeper shit than even he thought."

TWELVE

Sandy Dennis answered the door on my first ring. I hadn't called ahead because I wanted to catch her off-guard. One disadvantage of that strategy is the likelihood that she might think a guy my size means her harm.

Her ground-floor apartment had a glass storm door. I plastered a copy of my business card to the glass just to the side of the peephole, so she could see both it and me.

"What is it?" she asked, through the door.

"My name is Eamon Gold. I'm a private investigator. See the card? I'm working for Brandon Hunt."

"How do I know you're telling the truth?" she asked.

"You think anyone would willingly claim to work for him if they weren't? Look, if you don't believe me, call him."

"I think I will."

I cooled my heels on the porch, enjoying the crisp, cool morning air. Presently, I heard the multiple door locks rasp and clank. She opened the door.

She was shorter than I expected, not much more than five feet even. Her hair was dark, almost ebony, brushed flat to her skull and pulled to a tortuous ponytail that fell to mid-shoulders. I had been right. The purple hair was a wig. She invited me inside and offered me a glass of tea. Being the sociable type, I accepted.

"I assume this is about the blackmail note," she said.

"Partly. Doctor Hunt hired me for protection after he was assaulted the other evening. I assume you know about that."

"It's horrible. Who would want to hurt him?"

"Really?" I asked. "You want to start there?"

"Those critics...they don't know him. Half the shit he says is for shock value."

"So you think he's just a jolly prankster pulling the wool over liberals' eyes?"

"Are you going to twist everything I say?" she demanded. For an instant, I saw malice in her eyes, but she quickly recollected herself. "I'm sorry. Brandon might have told you. His weren't the only pictures they stole from my phone. I'm going through something of a bad patch right now."

"Are you being blackmailed as well?" I asked. "Because, if you are..."

"Are you offering a package deal?"

"Not necessary. I find out who's extorting Hunt, I find out who stole your pictures. You benefit whether you hire me or not. But, if these people aren't just targeting Hunt, that tells me something."

"Like what?"

"Perhaps they aren't ideological. It's just about money, at least in your case. That leads me in a different direction, detection-wise. Is someone trying to shake you down?"

She stared at me for a beat, and then retreated to the back of the house. She reappeared seconds later with a plastic essay folder. She took out a sheet of paper and laid it on the coffee table in front of me.

It read: *You should have better phone security. For $5000, we will destroy these files. We'll be in touch.*

"When did you receive this?" I asked.

"Three days ago."

"After Hunt was beaten up?"

"Yes."

"What do they have?" I asked.

She blushed, her ears cherry red, then she shook her head. "This is stupid. I know you've already seen the pictures sent to Brandon. Nothing to hide now. These are just same song, different lyrics."

I didn't tell her the sole picture of her with Hunt had hidden a lot more than it showed. I'll probably do some righteous burn time for that in the afterlife. I convinced myself I was just following a lead. I had, for instance, already learned that Brandon was holding out on me. There were more pictures than the one he had shared already.

She spread the photos out on the coffee table like a poker hand. Each one included a different partner—some male, some female. All of them featured Sandy performing acts that suggested she was punching way above her weight in the sack.

"I can see why you'd like to keep these off the street," I said.

"Actually, I'm still thinking it over," she said.

"Paying?"

"The whole thing. Kim Kardashian was a nobody until her sex tape came out. Now she's a multimillionaire. This may be more opportunity than threat."

I stifled the impulse to tell her that Kim Kardashian was the daughter of a man already rich and famous for defending O.J., among other things, and that Sandy was unlikely to find such fame just because some sexy pics hit the internet. It was only morning, far too early to ruin her entire day.

"Well, it's probably all academic anyway," I said. "I'm going to find the person who sent these and put them out of business. You want to get famous; you may need to find another way."

"How will you find them?"

"I am not inexperienced at this. Fact is, I may know who sent the letters later today or perhaps tomorrow. So, your window for notoriety is closing."

For an instant, I thought I saw her pout. Kids today.

"Why don't we start at the beginning?" I said. "I take it from these pictures that you and Hunt aren't...well..."

"Exclusive?" she finished. "Hell no. I mean, *ick*. He's twenty years older than me. We never even dated, really."

"He was a pickup?"

"Yeah. A friend and I were out at this neighborhood bar, and Brandon happened to be there. We knew each other, of course. I've taken several of his courses, and he's in my major department, so our paths had crossed a bunch of times. He caught my eye while I was at the bar waiting for a beer, and we started chatting. I'm working in Doctor Friedman's cognitive processes laboratory as a research assistant. He mostly wanted to talk about our current study at first, but slowly the conversation turned to other stuff."

"What stuff?"

"Sex stuff. We're studying cognitive differences between men and women, expanding on a landmark study from 1974 by a couple of researchers named Maccoby and Jacklin. Hunt doesn't like some of the data we're acquiring."

"Why?"

"He likes to believe women are inferior to men in every respect. Supports his male ego or something, I don't know. Anyway, part of the research regards gender identification as a factor in sexual attitudes and behaviors. Traditionally, women have been much more conservative regarding sex than men. Males of all mammalian species are openly promiscuous because it makes ethological sense. You guys can never be certain if an offspring is really yours, so you spread your seed hither and yon hoping for a bounty crop."

"Poetic," I said.

"Women are more selective, traditionally. They can only bear once a year, more or less, so they have to make every shot count. They search for the *best* partners. Males take any hole they can find."

"Not so poetic," I observed.

"The average male believes the optimum number of sexual partners in a lifetime to be about nineteen. The average female, four. At least, that's the traditional model. Doctor Friedman believes the information age has changed the dynamic. Her hypothesis is that male and female humans are now much more statistically similar in their sexual attitudes and behaviors than they were forty years ago. Like I said, we're updating the data."

I noticed, now that she was talking shop, she had relaxed and become more comfortable. She leaned back against the sofa cushions and waved her hands around as if lecturing a class, like she was transcribing a tape in her head.

"So, Hunt thought he'd test that hypothesis with you?" I said.

"Probably. He's never said as much. He sure came on to me, though. Asked if I could keep a secret, then told me he had some Extasy. Asked if I wanted any."

"Wait," I said. "*He* had the molly?"

"Yeah. He seemed kind of nervous about it at first, but I was game. We walked back over here, popped the tabs, and watched a movie on TV waiting for them to kick. We started feeling pretty good, and we fooled around a little."

"Whose idea was it to bring in a third player?"

"Mine. I know my way around a bed, but Brandon was interested in stuff that I didn't find appealing. Besides, he was having kind of a problem—you know, down there. I suggested getting things a little more crowded."

I pulled the picture Hunt had given me and placed it on the table. "Can you tell me who she is?" I said, pointing to the blonde.

"No. She was a Tinder date. I swiped right and it was on. She called herself Mandy, but a lot of people on Tinder use fake names."

"Why?"

"Lots of reasons. They're married but taking a walk on the wild side. They just read Erica Jong and want a zipless fuck. They don't want their private life to cross swords with their professional life. Take your pick. Probably as many reasons as there are people using fake names."

"But she called herself Mandy."

"Yeah."

"Mandy and Sandy?"

She shrugged.

"If you checked Tinder right now, do you think you could find her again?"

She chewed at her thumbnail for a moment.

"Gee," she said "I don't know. By the time I swiped on her, I was pretty fucked up. To tell you the truth, I don't really remember her face all that well."

"Let's try," I said.

Sandy grabbed her phone from the coffee table and opened the app. She swiped through profiles for what seemed like forever, until she stopped on one.

"This is her," she said, handing me the phone. The picture depicted a woman the right size and shape to be the blonde in the picture.

"This one says her name is Hyacinth."

She shrugged again. It seemed her default response to any argument. "Like I said, a lot of people use fake names on here. She probably changes hers every other day. But that's her. I remember her profile notes."

"She didn't say where she lived, by chance," I said.

"No, but she was here about ten minutes after I swiped her, so she can't be far away. Might even be on campus. One of the dorms."

I picked up Hunt's photo and slipped it back into my folder.

"Thanks," I said, standing. "You've been a big help."

"Are you going to talk to Mandy?" she asked.

"I'm going to try."

"You think she stole the photos in my phone?"

"It's a distinct possibility," I said.

"If she did, tell her something for me."

"What's that?"

"If she ripped off my phone, I'm gonna murder her Tinder rating." She sat back and crossed her arms.

"Ah, sweet revenge," I said.

THIRTEEN

Sonny sat on the bench outside Hunt's office when I arrived to relieve him.

"Any luck?" he said.

"Not too shabby. I found the blonde. Have a line on her Tinder profile. Speaking of which, how's it going with Earleen?"

"I called her," he said.

"And?"

"It was fun. And nice. Plan to call her again."

"I just love playing Cupid. Anything to report on Hunt?"

"Besides his obsessive-compulsive devotion to schedules?" Sonny said. "No. But tonight is his evening class. I don't think the guys who jumped him would be bold enough to do it again in broad daylight. If they plan to strike again, it will probably be then."

"Criminals fear the light," I said. "I think Batman said that."

"He was an incisive and perceptive head case. How do you plan to get up with the Tinder girl?"

"Probably going to set up a honeypot trap."

"What's that?"

"Oh," I said. "You're gonna love it."

I found Hunt sitting at his desk, his back to the door, staring out the window at the football stadium. He must have heard me step through the door and settle onto his sofa, but if he did, he showed no indication.

"Sandy Dennis says hi," I said. He started and whirled his desk chair around to face me.

"Gold! What the hell? How long have you been here?"

"Not long. I figured you must have seen me outside with Sonny."

"That's his name? Sonny?"

"I visited Sandy this morning. Did she tell you someone's shaking her down as well?"

He waved a dismissive hand in the air.

"Not my concern," he said. "Bigger fish to fry."

"You are a piece of work," I said.

"How so?"

"Well, to begin with, you lied to me," I said. "You told me Sandy offered you the Extasy. According to her, *you* had it."

"She's lying."

"Why?"

"What?"

"For what purpose? What does she have to gain? She's a coed, someone is extorting her to the tune of five large, and *she's* the one who's lying?"

75

"For all I know, she's in on it!" Hunt declared.

"I don't think so."

"Based on *what?* The claims of a half-blood mongrel slut?"

"That's one," I said. "You only get three before I walk. And I'm referring to the lie, but I'm considering taking a slice out of your hide for the racist shit as well."

He spun his chair around to stare out the window again.

"Jesus, I hate this city," he said.

"The animus is mutual, apparently," I said. "That's another thing bothering me. I can think of a dozen universities in the middle of this country who'd welcome a professor of your...um...political persuasion. Why stay in a bastion of Western liberalism?"

"You take the battle to the enemy," he said. "You don't hunker down in your safe space waiting for them to come for you."

"Wow," I said. "The paranoia is strong in this one. You think of people in this city as the enemy?"

"Liberals, multiculturalists, one-world-government proponents, economic globalists, sexual degenerates, miscegenists, the whole lot. This fucking city is an open-air market for the downfall of America."

"Say that again. I couldn't hear you through the pointy hood."

He turned the chair to face me and pointed toward the bandages on his face. "*This* is real. *This* is what happens when you try to be a patriot and uphold the vision of the framers of our Constitution."

"Funny. I thought your vision for this country had more in common with *Mein Kampf.*"

He sneered. "You're no better than the rest. It's obvious you have no personal investment in protecting me. Why am I paying you? As a matter of fact, I'm of a mind to fire you."

"A little late for that," I said.

"What do you mean?"

"I expect to know where your extortion note was printed in just a few hours."

He straightened in his chair.

"Really?"

"Certain brands of laser printers leave identifying marks on the sheets of paper. Your note was printed on one of them, sold to the university as part of a bulk purchase about a year ago. Later today, I anticipate finding out where it was allocated, and from there I can probably figure out who's blackmailing you. Of course, if you prefer to fire me, I'll just take all this information and walk away. Your choice."

Hunt leaned back in his chair. "I...I don't know what to say."

"As little as possible seems most appropriate. Oh, and I have a way to find the blonde woman in the picture as well, but if you're not interested..." I rose to walk out.

"Stop!" he said. I turned back and gave him the raised eyebrow. "...Please," he added.

"I have an errand to run," I said. "Can't be in two places at once, so you might want to stay put in your office until I get back."

"What about your partner? Sonny?"

"Right now, he's having lunch with a faculty member," I said. "I suppose he'll be back on his bench in an hour or so. Until then, cool your heels."

FOURTEEN

We tend to think of universities as ivy-covered halls filled entirely with sagacious professors and bright-eyed students. In fact, support and administrative staff at most universities outnumber academics by as much as three to one.

I had no idea who was responsible for the assignment and allocation of computer hardware on campus, so I started with the business office. There, I encountered a sturdy woman on the cusp of retirement named Bonnie Bartkowski. She wore a crisp business suit topped with a flouncy cravat, eyeglasses hanging on her chest with a thin gold chain, and an expression of skepticism. She raised her glasses to her eyes to examine my business card.

"A private investigator?" she asked.

"Don't tell me," I said. "You were expecting Efrem Zimbalist Junior."

"I wasn't expecting anyone. Nobody told me you were coming."

"That usually works better for me."

"Well, I'm extremely busy. What do you want?"

I pulled the sheet of paper Aubrey Innes had given me from my pocket. "I'm working for a faculty member who recently received some threatening communications. One of them came from a laser printer somewhere on this campus. I was hoping you could tell me where."

"I suppose you're working for Brandon Hunt," she said. She sniffed her disapproval.

"I'm not at liberty to divulge…"

"The man is a contemptible twit," she observed.

"On that we can agree."

"So why work for him?"

"I never said I was. However, if I were to take on Doctor Hunt's case, I can assure you that it would only be for the purpose of soaking him for every penny I can. I'm kind of mercenary that way."

"Yes," she said, drawing it out into hiss. "So, you want to know where the computer is?"

"This is correct."

"Hand me the paper."

I slid Aubrey's printout across her desk. She peered at it through the bottom of her bifocals.

"I can't tell you, of course," she said. "I only generate the purchase orders for these bulk acquisitions. You want the IT department. They handle the allocation of computers on campus."

"You know who runs it?" I asked.

"Of course. You want to talk to Farhad Sharif."

"Where can I find him?"

"At the moment, somewhere in Hawaii. He's on vacation until Monday."

"And you know this…how?" I asked.

"We're friends. When he gets back on Monday, he can tell you precisely where to find this nefarious printer."

"Nobody's available until then?"

"I'm sorry. He's kind of a one-man department. Besides, he hates Hunt more than I do."

"I can imagine why," I said.

"He's much more likely to help if I ask him. You and Hunt don't even need to come into the conversation. In my office, we have a vested interest in assuring the equipment we purchase doesn't go walkabout. I can just tell him we need a quick inventory check. He never asks questions of me."

"Why would you do that?" I asked.

She leaned forward. "To tell you the truth, even if you are working for that bastard Hunt, this is all kind of romantic and exciting."

"Precisely why I went into the business," I said.

I found Sonny on the bench outside Hunt's office again.

"Nice lunch?" I asked.

"Finest kind," he said.

"I can't find the printer until Monday. Guy's out of town."

"Somehow, I don't think you're telling me we get the weekend off."

"Yeah. You'll probably need to dump your Forty-Niners tickets. Want to help set up a honey pot?"

"Maybe, if you explain what it is," he said.

"Old Cold War trick. Still works. You find a mark who seems susceptible to seduction, bang his brains out, and then blackmail him with the pictures or video. Rather than admit to his superiors that he allowed himself to get sucked in by the enemy…"

"Literally," Sonny added.

"…The guy turns. What we're going to do is kind of like that. I have the blonde's Tinder account. We know she's up for spontaneous whoopie, so we create a fake account with the picture of a hunky guy whose profile is paraphrased to resemble her own."

"Birds of a feather."

"Precisely. When she shows up to throw down, we question her."

Sonny pulled his sunglasses from his shirt pocket and slipped them on. "You know there's another term for that these days. Kids call it 'catfishing'."

"Gotta love the kids," I said.

"I contacted some of my old buddies from the bad times," he said. "Asking around about muscle for hire."

"Come up with anything?"

"*Nada*. Of course, they were reticent to discuss their business affairs with me, ostensibly being on the side of the angels these days and everything."

"Reticent. Good word," I said.

"The straight skinny is nobody I know in the business hired out any guys to rough up Hunt. So, that's a dead end."

"Yet, they behaved like pros. What does that tell us, Watson?"

"They came from out of town, maybe."

"Possibly. What else?"

"We're working with a previously unknown bad guy," he said.

"Someone who has henchmen."

Hunt stepped outside his office building and crossed the sidewalk to us.

"I have to go do a class," he said. "One of you want to walk me?"

"Need me to carry your books too?" I asked.

He scowled. It wasn't pretty. "Do you have to make a snide remark about everything?"

"Turns out murder and assault are illegal," I said. "Sometimes, snide is all I have left in the toolbox." I handed Sonny a slip of paper with the blonde's Tinder information. "I'll take this. Why don't you head back to the barn and start working on that—what did you call it?"

"Catfishing," he said.

"Yeah, that. Work on the profile. Leave it on my desk, and I'll pick up on it soon as I finish with Mr. Chips here."

"Wait," Hunt protested. "Finish? Aren't you providing protection over the weekend?"

"Any time you aren't in your home," I said. "Just call my number a half hour before you go out, and one of us will be around. You might not see us, but we'll be there."

FIFTEEN

Sitting outside the building on a bench proved boring, so I slipped into the classroom again to see what kind of incendiaries Hunt might toss around. I sat in the back as I had before, because if I sat up front the next three rows wouldn't be able to see over my head.

The black kid who'd stomped out of class the other day sat a row in front of me, and about three seats down. He wore an SFSU letter jacket. I didn't know people still wore letter jackets after they left high school. I found it kind of quaint. Then I saw his hands as he took out his notebook. The knuckles were banged up, the way mine get after I go two or three rounds of bop the beezer with a bad guy. I switched seats to the one right behind him, and I dropped my business card on his notebook. He turned around. I could see surprise and a little fear in his eyes.

"Richardson, right?" I said.

"What about it?"

"Let's talk outside."

At first, I thought he might run. Instead, he stuffed his junk back into the bag and followed me out the door. I pointed to the bench near the front of the building.

"I don't have to talk to you, man," he said. "You aren't a real cop."

"The last guy I put in a hospital said the exact same thing."

"Are you threatening me?" he asked.

"Naw. Just establishing my credentials. This is the part where I ask what you were doing last Friday night, right around nine-thirty."

"Why should I talk to you?"

"Because the assault on Hunt is a criminal case, and real cops like to haul people downtown instead of relaxing in the sunshine on this bench. The inspector who pulled Hunt's beatdown is a buddy of mine. You convince me you weren't in on it, and I can save you a visit to an interrogation room. It's uncomfortable, the lights are garish, and they serve really awful coffee."

"What makes you think I had anything to do with that?" he demanded.

"Let's start with the easy stuff. What's your first name?"

"Anthony."

"That's what you go by?"

"Most people call me Tony."

"What sport do you play, Tony?"

"Baseball."

"What position?"

"Shortstop. I also wrestle. Why?"

"I played football here back in the days of leather helmets, before the university disbanded the program. Offense. Running back."

"No shit? You look more like a tackle."

"The years are short, but the mileage is staggering. You on a full ride?"

"Yeah. The works."

"Keeping up your grades is kind of important, right?" I asked.

He stared at the ground. "Yeah."

"So, you want to tell me why you left the class in a huff the other day?"

"You saw that?"

"Everyone saw that. And heard it. Two buildings over."

He pulled his bookbag onto his lap and hugged it closely. "You heard what Doctor Hunt said, too, then."

"I did."

"He basically said black people were born criminals."

"Yes," I said.

"Only so much a guy can take," he said. "I'd had a rough day already, and that was the last straw. I felt bad about it later."

"But it felt so good at the time."

He grinned. "Yeah. It did."

"I thought a lot about that little scene," I said. "Made me wonder. Forensic psych isn't exactly a creampuff course. I checked. It has a couple of tough prerequisites."

"And?"

"Not the kind of course your average jock takes."

He stared away from me, and I thought I saw tears form in his eyes. "All my fucking life, man...Look. Go down to the Records office. Check my transcript. Three years here,

86

and I'm still pulling a three-point-seven grade point average. I'm no average jock. I didn't come to college to play baseball. I play baseball—and wrestle—so I can come to college."

"Hunt was right when he said the only way you could get to college was through sports?"

"He said that? Well, he was right, but for the wrong reason. Money, man. We never had any. Sports are my ticket in, but I've done the work on my own. Most the guys on the team are dreaming of the MLB draft. A few might make it to the Double A leagues. I want more."

"Like what?"

"Thinking of being a psychologist. My advisor is Doctor Marley. You know her?"

"We've met."

"She says I have potential. She set me up with a lab assistant position with her partner, Dr. Friedman. She's planning to write me a reference letter for grad school."

I pointed to his barked knuckles. "Want to tell me how you got those?"

Tony tried to hide his hands, but they were too large. "I don't want to talk about that, man."

"Remember the stuff about garish lights and bad coffee?"

He seemed to deflate. After a heavy sigh, he said, "I got a chip on my shoulder. I know it. Been that way my whole life. I was at a kegger last weekend. Was talking to a cute white girl, and a guy made a crack. Some people can't get their head out of the nineteenth century. I asked if he wanted to take it outside. Turns out he did."

"Is this one of those *'You should see the other guy'* stories?" I asked.

"We both got our licks in, but it was mostly tussling and rolling in the dirt. I hit my hand on a tree. For real."

"Don't suppose you traded calling cards afterward. I wouldn't mind corroborating your story."

"It was all over in a few minutes, and I lost interest in the girl along the way. I went back to my dorm and watched TV until I fell asleep."

"Where was the party?"

"Frat house just off campus." He told me the Greek designation. I made a note to check it out.

"What time did you get there?"

"Around nine-thirty."

"And you left...?"

"I don't know. Ten, maybe."

"You're not sure?" I asked.

"I was preoccupied. I didn't check my phone. I guess that's not good for me, huh?"

"It could be better," I said.

SIXTEEN

Sonny and I decided to use his address for the ersatz hookup with Mandy/Hyacinth. My Russian Hill address is nice, but Sonny's is much sexier. The profile he placed in Tinder was a work of art—not surprising, since Sonny was an English lit major back in the day. He uploaded a picture I provided from my files, a nice professional headshot of Ty Cannon, a California surfer type who had dreams of being an actor. I didn't tell Sonny how Cannon looked when the police dragged his body out of a storm drain in Pacifica. Sonny called the avatar Moondoggie. I gave him the raised eyebrow treatment.

"She's way too young to get the reference," he said.

The prose couldn't have been a better match for her stated interests. Before uploading the profile, I ran it downstairs to Heidi's gallery to get a woman's opinion.

"I'd do him," she said. "Wait. Isn't that the kid from the storm drain?"

We let the profile sit overnight, ignoring a flurry of swipe-rights, while I watched over Hunt's evening class and escorted him to his car in the deck next to the fieldhouse. Nobody stopped us. Nobody even looked twice at us as we made the short trek from the psych building to his car.

Hunt wanted to run some errands on Saturday, so we took turns shadowing him from a safe distance. Around four in the afternoon, I told him to head back to his apartment so we could spring our trap.

We arrived at Sonny's place around six. I brought along a couple of foot-long Italian sandwiches from The Yellow Submarine. I didn't worry about the garlic and onions. We were going to interrogate the girl, not smooch with her.

We watched a movie while we ate our hoagies and chased them down with Anchor Steam, the beer that makes better detectives of us all. Around nine, we set our evil plan into action. Sonny opened his account and found Hyacinth/Sandy, who had already changed her name again to Bobbie.

"Here we go," Sonny said, and swiped right. Fifteen seconds later, his phone dinged.

"That was quick," I said.

"False alarm," Sonny said. "Someone just swiped on my profile. Nice looker. Way too young for me, though. Is it really this easy to get laid these days?"

"It's this easy to get chlamydia these days," I said. Then his phone dinged again.

"We're on," Sonny said. "It's her."

The girl arrived around ten, which—I have been assured—is the earliest *anyone* goes out these days. At my age, ten o'clock is when I usually wash down my Ambien with a glass of merlot. Ah, fleeting youth.

She knocked on the door. By plan, I waited in the back bedroom. Sonny was in the kitchen, out of view of the door.

"It's open," he called out. "Come on in. I'll be there in a second."

She walked in and surveyed the place like a real estate agent. Apparently, she approved. "Great place!" she called out.

Sonny returned from the kitchen, carrying a bowl of fresh guacamole dip and some tortilla chips. She examined him suspiciously.

"Moondoggie?" she asked. Her voice was pure San Fernando Valley. Not a local.

"No," he said. "I'm Sonny. Moondoggie's not here."

"What are you? Like, his dad?"

In the back bedroom, I stifled a snicker.

"No," Sonny said. He pulled out his business card and handed it to her. At the same time, I came down the hallway and stood behind her.

"A private detective?" she asked. "What is this?"

I cleared my throat, and she whirled around to look at me. I could tell she was about to freak.

"Relax," I said. "Nobody's going to hurt you. We just want to ask a few questions, and you can go. Try the guac. I had some a little while ago. Sonny makes the best."

While I distracted her, Sonny grabbed her purse from the coffee table and extracted her driver's license.

"And who are you?" she demanded. She pointed at Sonny. "*His* father?"

That stung a little. I don't mind admitting it.

"Name's Amy Beth Popowicz," Sonny said. "The license says she's from Pasadena."

"Hey!" she protested. "Give that back!"

"Absolutely," Sonny said. He snapped a picture of the license with his phone and handed it to her. He rifled a little more in the purse, coming up with an SFSU student ID, several packs of condoms, an iPhone, a small bottle of hand sanitizer, a lipstick, several miniature tubes of flavored lube, and a hairbrush. He held the student ID up to show me, then replaced all the other stuff and handed the purse back to Amy Beth. I slid the picture Brandon Hunt had given me onto the coffee table in front of her.

"Is this you?" I asked, knowing already that it was.

She took one glance at the photo and blanched. With her blonde hair, she looked like a panicked ghost.

"My name's Eamon Gold. I'm his employer." I pointed to Sonny.

"Partner," Sonny corrected.

"In training," I added. I handed her my card. "I'm working for Brandon Hunt."

"Who the fuck is Brandon Hunt?" she said.

I caught a quick warning glance from Sonny. He pointed to the picture. "This is Brandon Hunt. Is this you with him in the picture?"

I could tell she wanted to bolt. If she did, there wasn't much we could do to stop her, unless we wanted to court a kidnapping beef. I tried to put her at ease. I sat next to her on the sofa and dipped a chip into the guac.

"Your answer is kind of critical," I said. "You aren't in any trouble, as far as I know, but we need to know if this is you in the picture."

Finally, she nodded. "Yes," she said. "If I'm not in trouble, why are you asking?"

"Someone is trying to blackmail Doctor Hunt…"

"Wait," she said. "This is *Doctor* Hunt? The racist bastard in the psych department? I *fucked* that guy?"

Based on the picture, she'd done a darned sight more than that, but I didn't belabor the point.

"Honest," she said. "I didn't know who he was. The girl there, what was her name?"

"Sandy," I said.

"Yeah. Sandy. She invited me."

"Through your Tinder profile?" I asked.

"Yeah. She said she had some Ex and a boyfriend ready to play."

"She used the term *boyfriend?*" I asked.

"Yeah. I'll show you the message." She opened her phone's Tinder app, and scrolled down the page to her messages, then handed me the phone.

"Hi! You're hot!" the message said. *"My boyfriend and I are having a molly party. Want to join us?"*

I handed the phone back to her. "So you just went?"

"Sure," she said. "I love molly."

"Who doesn't?" Sonny said.

"I know! Right?" she said, her eyes lighting up. "You're pretty cool for an old guy. Big, too. You do 'roids?"

"All natural," Sonny said, smiling. "Like Mr. Gold said, Hunt is being blackmailed. We're eliminating suspects."

"Why do you think I'd do something like that?" she asked.

"These pictures were taken with Sandy's phone," I said.

"Who's Sandy?" she asked.

I pointed to the picture again. "That's Sandy. Remember? The girl who swiped you."

"Oh."

Sonny took over. I was fine with it. She seemed to respond better to him. "Someone stole this picture from Sandy's phone. You seemed like a promising suspect. If you don't mind, I'd like to look at the photos on your phone. Far as I'm concerned, if this isn't there, you're in the clear."

"Really?" she asked. "That's all?"

"Mr. Malehala has a keen eye for innocence," I said. I didn't say that, from what I could tell, innocence was not Amy Beth's strong suit. Her apparent genuine shock upon seeing the photo weighed against her being an extortionist, though, and I couldn't see her hiring a bunch of toughs to bounce Hunt off their fists a few times.

Sonny examined her phone, flipping through the pictures slowly and deliberately. He looked up at me and shook his head. He handed it back to her.

"You're clear to go," he said. "We're sorry we punked you, but it was the only way to find out who you were."

She quickly opened the Tinder app and switched her profile status to *'Available.'"*

"Need to update my status. Not getting laid here tonight." She looked back and forth at me and Sonny. "Am I?"

I handed her a twenty. "For gas and your trouble. Be careful out there, okay?"

Her telephone dinged. She glanced at it. "Yeah. Sure. Thanks for the money. Hope you find your blackmailer."

She held her hand up to her face like a phone receiver and mouthed *'Call me'* to Sonny. And she was out the door.

SEVENTEEN

Sonny had the Brandon Hunt watch on Sunday, which promised to be a slow day, so Heidi and I headed to my Montara house for a little R and R. After our Hawaiian trip the previous Christmas, she had recently taken up surfing and wanted to try out a new board she'd purchased. We packed a picnic, crossed the PCH, and spent the afternoon lazing on the beach. The day was warm, and the north end of the beach was largely deserted, so we set up there.

"Want to try?" she asked, as she zipped up her wetsuit. "It's really fun."

"I prefer water in its natural state—diluting scotch," I said. "I'll keep watch from here in case I need to call the Coast Guard."

She smiled, waved, and trotted out to the surf with her board. It wasn't a particularly rough sea that day, and she was likely to spend more time sitting on her board than catching any waves.

As she waited, bobbing up and down in the surf, I thought about the case. Nothing made any sense. I couldn't shake the inconsistencies. Hunt was being blackmailed. Hunt was attacked and beaten by a gang of toughs, something no extortionist would ever do. Hunt claimed Sandy had given him the molly, but Sandy said Hunt had it. Someone had stolen the pictures off Sandy's phone, but it wasn't Amy Beth Popowicz. Tony Richardson claimed he was in a tussle at a frat house the night Hunt was attacked but was really fuzzy on the time, and his battered knuckles suggested more than a casual pop at some tree bark.

A couple of possibilities came to mind.

The first was that I was working two different cases, one of which—the assault—Dexter Spears of the SFPD had warned me not to interfere with.

The other was that someone—or everyone—was lying to me.

I hate it when people lie to me.

Heidi caught a wave, paddled furiously to keep up with it, and then tried to stand on her board. She lasted about four seconds—a new record for her. I don't think she was interested in records. She just enjoyed the sea and the fresh air and sunshine. I kind of liked it as well. She crawled back on her board and paddled to the shallows, then carried it back to our blanket and buried the nose in the sand, like a Valkyrie Gidget. I poured some wine in a Solo cup and handed it to her.

"Sandwich?" I asked.

"Not yet. Might go back in."

"Might not."

She gazed up the beach and down to the other end. There was a lone beachcomber in the distance, too far away to be recognizable as anything other than an impressionistic stick figure.

"Might not," Heidi said. She turned her back to me, and I unzipped her wetsuit. Underneath, she wore a string bikini, and in a few moments, she didn't even wear that. She pulled a pump bottle of sunscreen from her bag and handed it to me. I did the honors.

"So, what's up with Sonny and Earleen?" she asked, as I painted her back.

"I think they are becoming an item," I said.

"Good. That makes me happy. We should have dinner with them soon."

"We also have an invitation to dine at Chez Panisse with Barbara Ledford and her boy toy."

"The high-priced spread," she said.

"The restaurant or the boy toy?"

"You know what I mean. I hope you make a lot of money off Brandon Hunt. You're going to need it."

"Barbara's treat. That program she and Rusty put together last year has made her a very wealthy woman. She wants to thank me for my contribution. In fact, she already did—a nice check with lots of zeroes."

Heidi raised her Solo cup. "Here's to gratitude."

She took the spray bottle from me and applied sunscreen to the front of her body. I sat back and admired her. Someday, somehow, we were going to have to take some time to figure out exactly who we were to each other. Today didn't seem like that time, though. I settled back on the blanket and propped myself up on one elbow.

"Something's bothering you," Heidi said, as she poured a little more wine into her cup.

"Just wool-gathering," I said. "Trying to fit all the pieces of this Brandon Hunt case together, and they aren't meshing."

"You're missing something."

"Wouldn't have any idea what it is, would you?"

"No. But you will. You always do. You poke and prod and bother people and get them all pissed off, and sooner or later someone tries to do something about that. And then, you know."

"Yes," I said. "It frequently works that way."

EIGHTEEN

Monday morning, I knocked on the door of the frat house just off campus where Tony Richardson claimed to have gone a few rounds with one of the brothers the night Hunt was attacked.

The knock was answered by a kid who looked about nineteen. He had longish extremely wavy brown hair, a cheesy excuse for a beard, and the reddest eyes I'd ever seen outside a vampire movie. I smelled burning rope from inside the house. The kid didn't seem to care.

"What?" he said.

I handed him my card. He stared at it for much longer than a college student should need to read it.

"Whoa," he said. "Five-Oh." He glanced back over his shoulder.

I shook my head. "Private cop. Relax. Besides, it's legal now."

"So, whaddaya want?" he asked.

"Need to talk to someone about the kegger you had a week ago Friday night."

"Hey man, we brought that keg back. I promise."

"This isn't about a keg. Can I come in? I don't like holding conversations in a doorway."

He shrugged, and I followed him into the living room. Like most frat houses, it was seedy, battered, and smelled of ancient yeast, stale weed, mold, socks worn far too many days in a row, and the faintest remnant of sex. Several Goodwill sofas were scattered about the massive main room, and about a hundred posters thumbtacked to the walls served as the primary decoration. A seventy inch flatscreen TV dominated one wall, with two or three video game consoles attached to it. If I were a nineteen-year-old stoner, it was the kind of place I'd love to call home.

"Were you at the party?" I asked.

He dropped onto one of the sofas and draped a leg over one of the arms. "Sure. Why?"

"I wanted to ask about a fight that took place that night."

He stared off into space for an instant, then his eyes lit up. "Oh! You want to talk to Mark!"

"Who's Mark?"

"The guy in the fight, dude. Hold on."

He hopped off the couch and headed upstairs, leaving me alone in the living room. I considered taking a seat, but decided I wasn't touching anything in that house without a tetanus booster. After a couple of minutes, I heard two sets of footsteps on the stairs. The stoner kid returned to the living room with another student, whom I presumed to be Mark.

"That's him," the kid said, and he left the room again.

"Mark?" I asked.

"Mark Ballenger," he said. He didn't extend his hand. He was close to six feet tall, with one of those builds you just knew was going to turn to suet in a few years. He was big but not fit, and his face was a little doughy. The most notable thing about him was his red hair, parted in the middle and falling over his ears on both sides.

I handed him my card.

"Yeah," he said. "Billy already showed it to me."

"First of all, you aren't in any trouble," I said. "I'm just following up on some information I received. Friday night last, you attended a keg party here at the frat, right?"

"Sure," he said. "Everyone here was at it."

"Fine. The kegger isn't a problem. I'm interested in the fight you had with Tony Richardson that evening."

"How'd you hear about that?"

"So you did fight him?"

"Since when do private investigators run around snooping about frat party fights?"

"When they take place at roughly the same time as an assault across campus. I'm clearing names."

"How did you get my name?"

"You just gave it to me. Tony told me about the fight. He said he threw down with one of the frat brothers here. Your pal eavesdropping from the top of the stairs told me it was you."

I heard padded footsteps walk away at the top of the stairs. Ballenger glanced in that direction, a sneer on his face.

"Teddy doesn't know what time it is. I don't think he makes a credible witness."

"You're sober as a judge, though, and you already tacitly admitted being in the fight."

"When?"

"When you said, *'How'd you hear about that?'* Look, if you want to be evasive, it's all the same to me. The assault I mentioned? It's still an open case with the SFPD. Why don't I just let the inspector handling that case talk with you?"

I stood and headed for the door. Ballenger stopped me before I left the living room.

"Wait. Okay. I got in a scrape that night. What about it?"

"Let's start with the fact you know Tony Richardson," I said.

"What about it?"

"You guys have some sort of history?"

"We know each other."

"What was the fight about?"

"A girl. What else?"

"What's her name?"

"Beats me. She was just some chick at the party."

"Student here at the college?"

"Yeah. I've seen her around."

"Now we're getting somewhere," I said. "What happened?"

Mark Ballenger sighed and allowed himself to settle back into the sofa cushion. "I saw her when she showed up at the party. Thought I might hit her up later, after she got a few beers in her."

"Not terribly chivalrous."

"Look around you. This place is where chivalry goes to die. Tony showed up later."

"What time?"

"I don't know, man. Later."

"Before or after nine-thirty?"

"That's when this assault took place?"

"What time did Tony show up? I gotta tell you, Mark, I'm getting tired of asking questions two and three times." I tried to make myself look mean as I said it. I gave him the scowl that weakens strong men's knees and turns their bowels to water.

"Between nine and ten, okay? Beyond that, I couldn't tell you."

I calculated the walking time from the Field House to the frat. Maybe ten minutes, on a leisurely stroll.

"And the fight?"

"I had a few beers myself, so my internal clock was kinda offline, y'know? Maybe ten minutes after he got here. Maybe fifteen. Maybe more. I don't really remember."

"And you fought over this girl whose name you didn't even know?"

"You said it earlier. Tony and me? We got a history."

"Tell me."

"He's a shortstop. I'm a shortstop. We both compete for the same position on the college baseball team."

"And he's a slightly better shortstop?"

"Coach thinks so. I had a bad day at tryouts."

"And in every day of spring training?"

"Okay. Tony's got an edge, all right?" he said. "Jeez."

"So you had a beef with him before he showed up that night."

"Yeah. I saw him hitting on that girl. Tony's not a frat member here. He had no business poaching on my territory."

"Poaching?"

"You know what I mean. Me and my brothers here bought the kegs. This is our turf."

"Giving you right of first refusal on the women who show up? Forget chivalry. This place sounds downright chauvinistic."

"Whatever, man. This is my house. Tony was a visitor. He should have shown respect."

"The same way he should have rolled over at baseball tryouts?"

"You're twisting my words."

"Can't resist. They're just so invitingly bendy. How'd the fight start?"

"I called him out. Told him I wanted a word. We went out back. I told him our welcome mat didn't apply to him anymore and asked him to leave."

"All right," I said. "Now tell me what really happened."

"You think I'm lying?"

"I think lying is your default. Tell me about how you sucker-punched him."

"Did Tony tell you that?" Ballenger said, his face growing red.

"You don't look like the type to wait around for someone else to make the first move."

He slapped at the couch arm and walked over to the window overlooking the front yard. He breathed heavily a few times and turned back to me.

"Okay. I walked him out back and gut-punched him as soon as we got to the bottom of the stairs. Are you happy?"

"That didn't end it?"

"Tony's tougher than I thought. We got into it. Tussled around on the ground for a couple of minutes. Tossed a few punches each. Nothing landed hard."

"The scabs on your knuckles suggest otherwise."

He chuckled. "Those? Shit, man. In the middle of it all, I hit a tree."

"With both hands?"

"Like I said, I'd had a few beers. Why?"

"Nothing. Just seems to be a lot of tree-punching going on lately."

NINETEEN

I caught up with Sonny on a bench outside Hunt's office. He had dispensed with the Joe College getup, and instead wore a pair of 501 jeans, some Doc Martins, and a plaid flannel shirt with the sleeves rolled. He was reading a copy of *Atlas Shrugged*, but he looked up as I neared.

"Really?" I pointed at the book.

"Stole it off Hunt's desk," he said. "I got an English degree, but somehow I never ran across this literary gem."

"There's always grad school. What do you think?"

"Man, there is some seriously fucked-up shit in here."

"I do believe that's a direct quote from the review in the *New York Times.*"

I sat on the bench next to him.

"Solve the case yet?" he asked, without looking up from the book.

"There's no case to solve. We've been warned off the assault, remember? Inspector Dexter Spears has everything under control."

"If I were drinking milk right now, it would be squirting out my nose," he said. "What about the blackmail?"

"Not officially our case."

"But you're snooping around it anyway."

"Technically, *we're* snooping around it. The more I learn, though, the stranger it all becomes."

"How so?"

"You ever run across two guys who saw a fight between them exactly the same way?" I asked.

"Never."

"Me either. Tony Richardson's primary alibi for not kicking the shit out of Hunt is that he was busy kicking the shit out of some other guy at a frat house across campus at the time."

"Gotta give him points for creativity. Most guys just say they were at home in bed."

"But, get this. I interviewed the other guy this morning. Kid named Ballenger. He told me the exact same story Tony did."

Sonny closed the book. "Do tell?"

"Right down to punching a tree during the melee."

"Melee. Good word." Sonny said. "So, both of them said they punched a tree?"

"Yeah."

"I miss college keggers. Those were the days. Night was never complete unless you tossed a couple of haymakers at a sugar maple. You think they cooked up their stories together, and just forgot who punched what?"

"I'm saying it's strange. Like everything else in this case."

"Don't tell me. The timing of the fight gave them exactly enough time to get from the field house to the frat house."

"Another fact that troubles me."

"We'll figure it out," he said. "That's why they pay us the big bucks." He glanced at his watch and took to his feet. "You on the clock? Thought I'd drop by Earleen Marley's office, see if she wants to go to lunch."

"Sure," I said. "Say hi for me. You guys are spending a lot of time with each other lately."

"She's very classy. I like that. Her shower has much better water pressure than mine, too."

I looked up at him. He winked. I love it when a good plan comes together. "Hunt's next class is at one-thirty. Be back by then if you can. I'm expecting a call from the head of the IT department."

As if on cue, my cell phone vibrated. I checked the caller ID. Farhad Sharif. I waved Sonny off and answered the phone.

"Mr. Sharif," I said. "I was hoping to hear from you today."

"I've been on vacation," he said, in a sophisticated Oxford accent. "I just returned to my office after a morning meeting and found a note from Bonnie Bartkowski saying I should call you. What's this about?"

I explained that I was working for a faculty member who was being blackmailed, and the note came from a printer on campus.

"Blackmail!" he said. "Oh, my. I don't suppose your client is Brandon Hunt."

"Confidentiality forbids, I'm afraid. Out of curiosity, why did you jump to that conclusion?"

"I'd imagine he's probably the most blackmailable faculty member on campus."

"Are you going to be in your office this afternoon, say around one-forty-five?"

"I should be," Sharif said.

"I'm on a stakeout right now," I said.

"My. How fascinating."

"Yeah. It's a real blast. I'm free around one-thirty. I'd like to drop by your office to discuss this further."

"By all means," he said. He gave me the building and office number.

"Oh," I added. "If I give you the serial number of a printer, can you find out where it's been deployed on campus?"

"Certainly. I keep all the logs in my office."

I read off the serial number, and we agreed again to meet after Sonny returned from lunch. I had an hour and a half to kill. I settled back on the bench and tried to make all the loose ends in this case come together. It was like putting socks on an octopus.

TWENTY

Farhad Sharif was a bantam of a man in his late thirties. He came chest-high on me, but he was obviously fit, judging by his flat belly and the way his biceps stretched the arms of his knit college pullover. His neck was a mass of veins and muscle. His face was dark, with a sharp nose and full lips surrounded by a meticulously trimmed goatee. His jet black hair was combed straight back into a ponytail that fell halfway down his shoulder blades. Despite persistent caffeine jitters, he clearly took great pains to put forward the most elegantly rebellious image.

Sharif's office, in comparison, was a war zone. Books were strewn everywhere. Dust a millimeter thick lined the shelf under his window. A long workbench installed against one entire wall contained various pieces of computer hardware in various states of disrepair. His desk was dominated by three monstrous computer screens, a half-eaten turkey sub, and what appeared to be a plastic beach bucket full of soda. The place smelled like stale coffee and fried circuits. He rose from his chair the instant I rapped on his open office door.

"Mr. Gold?" he said, his eyes gleaming.

I handed him my business card.

"A private investigator," he said. "I can honestly say I have never met a person in your profession."

"That you know of," I said.

He tilted his head in confusion for an instant, and then grinned widely.

"Yes! Who knows? Perhaps I have! Please, have a seat and tell me all about this blackmail case. I'm fascinated."

Sharif grabbed an armful of technical journals from a battered green pleather love seat and gestured for me to sit. He returned to his desk.

"Mind if I eat while we talk?" he said. "I had a faculty meeting run long, and I'm teaching an HTML coding course in a half hour."

I realized, between my meeting with Mark Ballenger and Sonny deserting me for a rendezvous with Earleen, I hadn't eaten. I slipped a late lunch into my mental agenda right between meeting with Sharif, and whatever it led to.

"Sure. Go right ahead." He picked up the sandwich and took a large bite, chewing intently as I said, "I can't tell you a lot. The blackmail note sent to my client contained machine code, which provided the serial number of the printer. I was able to trace that serial number to a consignment of printers purchased by the college. I just need to know where I can find that printer."

"Come on," he said. "It's Brandon Hunt, right?"

I pointed to my business card on his desk. "See? Right under my name. It says *Discreet Investigations.* If I run around town blabbing about my clients, I'll have to order new cards. That's overhead. I hate overhead. You cruise a lot of porn sites, Professor?"

"I don't see where that's any of—"

"You're right. It isn't. I don't care one way or the other, for that matter. Some people might. If you were my client, they wouldn't learn about it from me. I'm kind of like a priest. People tell me their secrets, and I keep them that way."

"I see," Sharif said.

"Mostly," I added. I grinned a little.

"Some secrets are hard to keep."

"Some aren't. This is one of them. I can't talk about my client. But now I'm intrigued. I'm familiar with Dr. Hunt, of course. Anyone who follows the local news is. That's the second time you've suggested I might be working for him. On the phone, you said he was the most blackmailable person on campus."

"I did."

"Mind if I ask why?"

"Curiosity?"

"Sure. That curiosity is powerful stuff. Besides, my current case won't last forever. Sooner or later, I'll need to scare up some new business. He sounds like a good place to start."

"If he's being blackmailed, of course."

"Goes without saying," I agreed. "So, why would someone blackmail him?"

"Besides being an insufferably horrid human being? Sex stuff, mostly. Some drugs."

"And you know this...how?"

"I'm in IT. We deal in information. Most of the end user dealers in town are computer science students. Keeps 'em in Cheetos and the latest game consoles. They talk, too. The cultural image of the IT nerd is an exaggeration, but not by much. Lotta kids on the spectrum wind up in this field."

"The spectrum," I said.

"You know. The autistic spectrum. I mean, it's not universal, but we get a lot more than our share. There are different rules online, rules more amenable to people who have problems dealing with skinware."

"Skinware being—"

"Other people. For some folks, avatars are a lot less threatening. They blab a lot, and they aren't really interested in other people's privacy, including who's buying what from whom. People like Hunt."

"You don't like Hunt?"

He chuckled. "At some level, I admire the son of a bitch. College campuses are closed communities. You gotta go along to get along, unless you favor the idea of retiring as an assistant professor—or worse, not getting tenure at all. A little iconoclasm is respectable and tolerated, but actually rocking the boat is frowned on."

"And Hunt rocks the boat."

"He gets away with it," Sharif said. "That's what's aggravating. He says the most godawful shit, and he skates. Chutzpah like that, you gotta admire."

"But when you take off your fanboy hat?" I said.

"Doctor Hate? I'd pay cash money to see the motherfucker go down." He emphasized the remark with a sizable slurp from the monster soda on his desk.

"You know he was attacked on campus a few nights back?"

"What? No shit? For real?" Sharif appeared elated. "Sorry. I didn't know. Honest. I've been on vacation for the last week and a half."

"Hawaii,"

"Right! My first day back. Wow. You really are a detective."

"Good memory. Bonnie Bartkowski mentioned it last week. Also, common frame of reference. My sweetie and I took a trip there last Christmas. You just said you'd love to see Hunt go down…"

"Wait. Who attacked him?"

"Beats me." Which was largely correct. "It's a police case. I'm not involved." Which was only tangentially correct.

"They fuck him up pretty good?"

"He's still teaching. Barely missed a day. Guess they just roughed him up."

"Too bad." He took another bite of his sandwich to stifle his tears.

"Like I was saying, if you want Hunt to go down, it sounds to me like your students hold the key to that."

"For scoring some weed and a little molly now and then?" Sharif said. He snorted. "Dude, if you handed walking papers to every faculty and staff member who smokes ganja or pops the occasional tab, the parking lot attendants would be teaching the courses. As long as we show up and get the job done, recreational body chemistry modification is ignored."

"That leaves the sex thing."

"You don't rock the boat and you don't bang the coeds," Sharif said. "Cardinal rules nowadays. Wasn't always that way, but times change, and this time it was for the better. I'm not saying that kind of stuff doesn't happen. College campuses are loaded with energetic young women with daddy issues, and professor-student trysts are damn near cultural archetypes. Those few who still choose to die on that hill tend to keep it on the down low. Hunt is reckless. Maybe it's part of his macho fascist world view, but he doesn't seem to care that people see him in public carousing with students. Maybe winning that lawsuit made him invincible to traditional faculty discipline. All I know is, the back-channel chatter suggests Hunt knocks off more covert coed nookie than any five other professors."

"Sounds like a motive for blackmail," I said.

"Which makes him the most blackmailable professor on campus. So, when you said you were working on a blackmail case—"

"And we've come full circle," I said. "Have you had a chance to track down that printer serial number?"

"I have," he said. He handed me a slip of paper. "It's assigned to a public computer lab in the student center."

"Public? How public?"

"You can walk in right now and be online in five minutes. Three if you have a student ID."

"Anyone's allowed to use it?"

"Yeah."

"Student or not?"

"Anyone means anyone. Guy who runs the lab is one of my grad students, kid named Owensby. I wrote his name on the slip as well. I gotta tell you, though, it would be hard for you to pick a worse location to identify a user. The traffic in that place is wicked mad."

TWENTY-ONE

Carl Owensby was tall, lanky, and loose-limbed. His shaven head and neck beard were intended to look at once hipster and intimidating, but only accented his low relative standing on the food chain. He wore an Alabama Shakes tee shirt, ratty jeans, and sparkling new sneaks. I found him in the student center computer lab, loading paper into a laser printer the size of a small refrigerator. I handed him my card. He peered at it through coke-bottle glasses.

"'kay," he said.

I waited for him to say something else. Most people do. I suppose Carl Owensby wasn't just some people. I showed him the slip of paper Farhad Sharif had given me.

"I'm looking for the printer with this serial number," I said.

"'kay," he said. He loaded another ream of paper. I waited for him to finish. He shut the hopper door, straightened up, and walked back to the main desk. I followed. He looked at me as if seeing me for the first time. "Help you?"

"Yes, as a matter of fact," I said. "I was hoping you'd help find this machine."

"Man," he said. "I just keep 'em loaded with paper. I don't know 'em by name. The printers are over there. You're welcome to check the serial numbers on the back."

He turned his attention to a computer screen and started tapping at a keyboard, his interest in me apparently satisfied.

I'd seen the printer on Barbara Ledford's desk, which was the same model as the one I was looking for, so I was able to quickly eliminate all but a trio of printers on a side table. It took me fifteen seconds to deduce that the one in the center was my quarry. I imagine it was supposed to be some kind of *Aha!* moment, but I immediately felt like the dog who finally caught the car. What to do with it now?

I had the date and time the blackmail note was printed. I looked around the lab. It was roughly forty feet by fifty feet, jam-packed with computer terminals, about seventy-five percent of which were occupied at three o'clock in the afternoon. There might have been forty people clacking away or cruising websites.

I returned to the front desk and Carl Owensby, who stared at the computer screen in front of him as if it might harbor the secret to eternal life. I rapped my knuckles on the countertop to get his attention.

"Find your printer?" He didn't look away from the screen.

"Yes."

"'kay." It had the sound of finality.

"Could I ask you a few questions?"

For an instant, he glared at me. That is not an exaggeration.

"Doctor Farhad Sharif said I could count on you," I added. The effect was immediate. Owensby obviously wasn't averse to pleasing his department head. I had his rapt attention, which in his case meant he only spent half his time staring at the computer screen. "Is there a way to find out who was logged into which computer station at a specific day and time?"

I'd used too many words. Owensby stared long enough for me to wonder if he was having an absence seizure. Finally, he shook his head.

"No," he said, and turned his attention back to the screen.

"Why not?" I said.

"Can't do it here, dude," he said, without looking up. "Everyone logs on with their student ID. We don't keep those sorts of records here."

"Who does?"

He spun his office chair in my direction and gave me a look of pure malice for making him deal with dumb skinware. "Nobody. Not really. I mean, I'm sure there's a file somewhere in the IT department of every login on every computer in the college. But it would be raw data. It wouldn't be like a list or nothing."

"Non-students use the lab too, though, right?"

"Sure. Each station has a credit card reader."

"But the college doesn't store those records either, I suppose?"

"Not our issue, as long as the checks from the credit card companies clear. Stuff like paid computer time and copying are big line items in the college budget."

I gave him the date and time Hunt's blackmail note had printed. "Were you working then?"

He froze up again. After a few seconds, he nodded. "Yeah. That was one of my shifts."

"Do you remember that shift at all?"

"Not really, man. After a while, they all run together."

"But you don't recall anyone acting shifty, or overly nervous, or anything like that?"

He shook his head. "I'm just here to keep the printers loaded and assist with malfunctions. Otherwise, this place pretty much runs itself. Most of the time, I don't even know these people are here."

TWENTY-TWO

The afternoon wasn't a total loss. The student center computer lab was situated directly across from the food court, and I still hadn't eaten. I ordered a garbage slice and a soda, and a small side salad to assuage my guilt over the pizza.

I found an empty table and took a seat. As I munched on the pizza and ignored the salad, I looked around. The campus had changed dramatically since my days as a student there. Some parts, I barely recognized. The students were remarkably young as well. I like to think I'm still just at halftime in my life, and I was only a couple of decades and change away from college myself, but these kids just looked like kindergartners. Most of them bopped around the union with the bright-eyed eager faces you're blessed with before life kicks the living shit out of you. These kids were oblivious to the shellshock waiting for them, and for that I envied them a little.

My table was next to a room divider and a fake potted palm, so when Tony Richardson entered the food court, he didn't see me. I saw him, though. I took another bite of pizza and watched him. He didn't do the usual tour of the court, examining each food joint before settling on the one he wanted. Instead, he stood at the entrance, his hands in the pockets of his letter jacket, and he surveyed the room as if looking for someone. This went on for a couple of minutes, and then he shrugged and grabbed a sub at one of the vendors. He sat diagonally from me, on the other side of the food court.

He reminded me of the problem I had with the matching stories from him and Mark Ballenger. Sonny had caught on to the implication immediately. There are always two sides to every story and to every fistfight. Nobody ever sees themselves as the aggressor, the instigator. For some guys, there's always a ready excuse for stuffing a two-by-four up some bastard's ass. Some guys wake up each morning with no other desire than to jam someone else up, and they walk around all day looking for candidates. Some other guys are like natural fight magnets. They aren't intentionally violent themselves, but they have the uncanny ability to piss off people and bring out the worst in others. Put these two guys together, and the only thing left is to take bets on the fight.

That wasn't the case with Ballenger and Richardson, though. Ballenger admitted to a legitimate grudge against Richardson, for taking a starting position Ballenger believed belonged to him. Richardson, on the other hand, still believed the fight was over the girl he chatted up at the party. Ballenger stuck with that story as well, at least at first. Maybe the part about fighting for the shortstop spot was an embellishment. The kicker, though, was both boys claiming their knuckles were scabbed over because they punched a tree. I've seen some clumsy barfights in my time, but it takes a special kind of inept, maladroit pair of brawlers to hit the same tree during a scrabble. Their stories wouldn't flush.

Tony put his sandwich down and looked toward the food court entrance. I followed his gaze and was almost surprised to see Mark Ballenger. Ballenger waved at Tony before buying a slice at the Sbarro and joining him at his table. Neither of them looked particularly angry or surly toward the other. On the other hand, they didn't look like buddies, either. They talked quietly and earnestly. They looked, more than anything else, like conspirators.

I would have loved to know the content of their conversation. Failing that, I thought it might be fun to rattle their cage a little. I looked up at the ceiling as I mused on my next move, and I saw a series of dark plastic half-spheres embedded in the ceiling tiles. Security cameras. Several of them had clear views of the computer lab. An idea formed in my head. First, though, I thought I might stir the pot a little, see what bubbled to the top.

I finished my lunch, dumped the refuse in the recycle bin, and walked directly over to the table where Richardson and Ballenger sat, still focused on their intense conversation. Tony saw me first. The look on his face was priceless. It took a lot of willpower to stifle my snicker.

"Mr. Gold!" he said.

Ballenger turned toward me. I didn't hear the word, but his lips clearly formed the word *shit*.

"Hi, guys!" I said, as I pulled up a chair. "How's it hangin'?"

I'm in the information business. I learn a lot just by asking questions. Sometimes, though, you make better headway by shaking the trees to see if anything drops out. If nothing else, maybe you piss off the right people, and they try to do something about it. As long as I'm prepared for it, they're welcome to try. Either way, you learn something using that strategy as well.

"It's good to see you two bury the hatchet," I said.

Ballenger's face flushed, and I knew I had him.

"Uh, I got a class," he said, and pushed the chair from the table.

"Oh, it'll wait a minute or so. I just had a couple more questions, and with both of you here I can get it all out of the way with one blow."

I accented the sentence by slapping my palm onto the tabletop, but I never took my eyes off their faces. Both flinched. I love it when they flinch. It means I'm close to some truth for a change.

"First, let me put your minds at ease," I said, knowing full well that I would do nothing of the kind. "That fight the other night? There are literally no discrepancies between your stories. Do you have any idea how rare that is? I must spend half my time on a case trying to figure out which person in a dispute is lying to me. In your case? No problem! Your accounts match up remarkably. So, thanks. You've saved me a lot of time and effort. I appreciate it."

Ballenger started to relax. I could tell Tony was still suspicious.

"I just need a few more details, and you guys are done with me." They weren't, but it served my purposes to let them think they were. "The girl. I need her name."

"The girl?" Ballenger said.

"Yeah. You know. The girl you guys went to the mattresses over." I turned to Ballenger. "The stoner kid who answered your door —Teddy?— confirmed he saw you fight Tony here at the kegger."

"Okay," Ballenger said. "So why do you need the girl's name?"

"Loose ends, Mark. They look sloppy on a final case report. I've known a lot of women in my time, and I never met one who wasn't impressed by a couple of guys fighting over her. Must be in the genes, you know? Probably goes all the way back to cavemen. Mating competition is a hallmark of nature. I just need to confirm with her that she knew you were fighting over her, and that'll be that."

"I never got her name," Tony said. "I barely said two sentences to her before Mark went ballistic."

"And you'd been at the party for how long before the fight?"

"I just got there," Tony said. "I literally walked in, grabbed a cup of beer, saw the girl, and started a conversation with her. Maybe five minutes. Maybe less."

"That's right," Ballenger said. "I saw him walk in. Maybe three minutes."

"Might want to look into anger management there, Mark. That's a really short fuse you got there," I said. I turned to Tony Richardson. "You know what this is all about, right? I mean, you guys hashed everything out."

"Uh, yeah. Sure," Ballenger said. I'd heard grooms at shotgun weddings speak with greater confidence.

"So, you're okay with that?" I asked Tony. "Mark here being upset because you beat him out for shortstop?"

Tony shot Ballenger a look that suggested the baseball story had been exactly as I suspected—an embellishment. Tony recovered quickly and nodded.

"Yeah. Water under the bridge."

"Great to hear it. So, if you'd give me the young lady's name, Mark, I can get out of your hair."

I've been in the reading people biz for maybe a quarter century. Either Mark was shining me on about the girl, or he didn't want to tell me her name for another reason. I had him pinned against the ropes, though. He wasn't getting rid of me until he gave her up, and he knew it.

"Her name's Amy," he said, after a couple of glances at Tony. "Amy Popowicz."

Sometimes, even a grizzled veteran cop like me catches a surprise that makes my heart skip a beat.

"Amy Beth Popowicz from Pasadena?" I asked.

"Yeah," Ballenger said. "You know her?"

"We've met," I said.

"You and a lot of other guys," Ballenger said. "Amy's kind of...um..."

"We used to say *easy*," I said.

"I was going to say *a ho*."

"Of course you were. Why didn't you tell me her name when we talked the other day?"

"You didn't ask. I decided to keep her name out of it."

"You're pretty tight with her, then?"

"Not really," Ballenger said. "But I wanted to be that night."

"Enough to go three rounds with Tony? Sounds like you were really hard up."

"Midterms, man. Had to decompress. I walked in, saw Amy at the keg, and figured my night got made. Then Tony started to horn in on my action."

"And it ended in tears. So you invited Tony out back, sucker-punched him, and discovered he was made of stronger stuff than you expected. At which point did the tree get jumped into the fight?"

They looked at each other, and back at me. Tony glanced at his abraded and scabbed knuckles.

"Different times," Ballenger said, a little too facilely. "I took a swing at him and missed. We tussled a little and he backed me up to the tree and took a slug at me and missed."

"How'd the fight end?"

"We just ran out of steam," Tony said. "It ain't like on television."

"No," I said. "It ain't."

"I figured I wasn't wanted around there anymore, so I went home," Tony said. "Not even sure why I fought in the first place. I was just talking with that Amy girl. Doesn't mean I wanted her that way. Maybe I figured it was time Mark and I got things straight. Get rid of the tension."

"Over the starting shortstop thing," I said.

"Sure," Tony said.

I turned to Ballenger. "So, Tony went home, and what happened then?"

He looked confused. "What do you mean?"

"Faint heart never won fair maiden, and you'd just gone to battle over Amy. How'd it turn out with you and her?"

"Um…"

"Never mind," I said. "I'm sure she'll fill in the details. But that reminds me of something else. Mark, you said you walked into the room and saw Amy Popowicz at the keg?"

"Yeah?" Ballenger said.

"Where were you before that?"

"What?"

"Before you walked into the room and saw Amy."

"I don't understand the question."

"You walked into the room and saw Amy. Immediately, Tony walked through the door, went to the keg, and talked to her. So, we know Tony was outside, approaching the frat house just as you came into the room. Where were you before that? And please don't ask me to elaborate further. You were somewhere just before the confrontation with Tony."

"I was…hell, I don't remember. Probably in the kitchen."

"Alone?"

"No. People gather in there. It's where we keep the snacks."

"Did you talk to anyone in particular in the kitchen?"

"Sure. I mean, probably. I don't recall it so well. I'd had a few myself, already."

"Let's say I offered you a million dollars cash to name one person you talked to in the kitchen for more than a couple minutes. Could you come up with a name then?"

"I suppose. But I'd have to think about it. I was a little drunk, and I talked to a lot of people that night. I just can't recall who I spoke with and when."

"Probably not important anyway," I said. "Just a thought. Nice to talk to you guys."

I pushed my chair away and stood to leave. I could almost feel them relax. It was time to hit them with the stinger. I walked a few paces away, stopped, rubbed my chin, and turned back to them.

"You know," I said. "I still can't get over it. Your accounts of the fight. It's refreshing. You just mentioned the tension between you. I can see it. Yet, you two were able to think beyond your personal grievances, and not scapegoat one another. That's admirable. Your stories were one hundred percent consistent. I mean—" I chuckled and shook my head. "—it's almost like you cooked it up together. But that's ridiculous, right?"

I chuckled again and exited the food court.

TWENTY-THREE

"You still have that picture of Amy Beth Popowicz's ID in your phone?" I asked Sonny as I walked up to him. He sat on the bench outside Hunt's office.

"Sure. Why?"

"Send it to me. I need to talk to her, and I don't think she'll fall for the honeypot trap again."

"I don't know," he said. "She was pretty dumb. What's going on?"

"She's popped up again. Those two knuckleheads at the frat house were fighting over her."

"And, right now, they're your prime suspects in Hunt's beatdown by the fieldhouse?"

"They smell good for it."

Sonny crossed his arms over his chest. "Coincidences suck."

"I have taught you well, padawan."

"You want to throttle back on the master-student bullshit? It's wearing thin."

"Once I can get back here and shake you loose from babysitting Hunt, I need you to do a stakeout on Mark Ballenger."

"The frat boy?"

"I get a weird vibe from him. I think Tony Richardson is involved in some way, but Ballenger acts like he's in charge. Besides, Richardson didn't know Amy Beth Popowicz's name and Ballenger did. So, if she's involved, he's a better candidate for observation."

"Involved in what?" Sonny asked. "What the fuck's going on here, Eamon?"

"Excellent question. All I know is, things aren't what they seem. For now, it's still just a blackmail case. All this other stuff, though..."

What's the word on the printer?"

"Probably a dead end. I might check with Doctor Sharif again, see if he knows a way to tease the user logs out of the college data system, but right now it doesn't look good. There may be an alternative, though."

"What's that?"

"The student center has security cameras in the ceiling, some with a view of the computer lab. If I'm really, really lucky, one of them might have caught the person who printed the blackmail note."

"So, all you have to do is convince the campus cops to let you examine their recordings."

"Right now, it's all kind of conceptual. I'm still chewing over the details. I'm just a blue collar peeper. The college security is under no obligation to indulge my fishing expedition just because I flash my expensive business card. Like one of the knuckleheads said today, it ain't like television."

"No. It ain't," Sonny repeated. "Maybe they aren't so dumb after all."

"I think they're plenty smart. You good here for another hour or so?"

"Sure. Billable hours. The beast must be fed. Why?"

"I'm headed downtown. Might do a little horse trading."

Dexter Spears did not look joyful when I walked into his cubicle at the SFPD.

"Gold," he said. "What are you doing here?"

"I come bearing gifts. Where are you on the Brandon Hunt assault?"

"Why should I tell you?"

"In the course of providing services to Dr. Hunt, I've run across some stuff. I don't want to interlope on your turf, you see. I have a couple of names to trade."

"What do you want in return?"

"I need access to the security tapes of the fieldhouse the night Hunt was jumped. I also need to get some footage of the computer lab in the student union."

Spears settled back in his chair and placed his hands behind his head. He peered down his nose at me. He thought it was disarming. It wasn't. Guile was evidently not his strong suit.

"You're not working the assault, are you?"

"Only tangentially. It's not my prime focus. There are other events taking place in Hunt's life that he prefers not to bring to the police."

"Why?"

"Probably because he thinks you haven't done shit about finding the guys who tossed his salad, and he believes you'd just as soon toss him into the big shredder and feed the pieces in the small one."

"He isn't far off," Spears said. "But the job's the job, right?"

"That's what Frank Raymond used to say. But he was dirty."

Right after Spears sort of earned his gold shield, Frank Raymond was his first partner. Frank had also been my partner when I was on the city payroll. The last I saw Frank, he stood in the circle of an overhead mercury lamp in an Alameda industrial park, surrounded by armed tong soldiers, after betraying Chinatown boss Sung Chow Li. He was seconds away from boarding the offworld shuttle, and he knew it. I saw the terror in his eyes. Walking away was the hardest thing I ever did, and the memory kept me awake at night. My only comfort was knowing Frank would have done exactly the same if our situations were reversed, and he wouldn't have lost a minute of sleep afterward.

Even though he was only a rookie partner, Spears caught some of the shrapnel in the aftermath, especially when Chinatown erupted into a full-fledged tong war. He didn't like being reminded of Raymond. The random pairing had tarnished his budding nepotistic career.

"I can't give you the video, but what we have is a copy anyway. Campus security still has the original. I can call the chief up there and formally request he give you access. In the interest of good interdepartmental relations, I'm sure he'll agree. As to the computer lab stuff, you can negotiate that with him. It's not part of my case."

"It might be, but I can't tell you why."

"You don't want to withhold evidence, Gold. That shit won't flush around here."

"I'm here to give you what I know. You want it or not?"

He stared at me, his face contorted in mixed emotions. Maybe it was ulcers. Finally, he said, "Whatcha got?"

"Make the call first," I said.

"What?"

"The security guy. Ask him to let me see the video."

"For real?"

"Yes. It'll take you a minute, and what I have could solve your case."

More staring. I resisted the urge to pull out my Swiss Army knife and clean my nails. Spears picked up the phone and dialed some numbers. After a few pleasantries, he said, "Got a guy in my office, private cop here in town, who's providing...um...material evidence in the Brandon Hunt assault. He needs to...corroborate his information by comparing it to the security videos you collected."

I rolled my index finger in the air, and mouthed *Aaaaand?*

Spears scowled, but said, "And he'd like to examine some video of a computer lab. It might be related."

He nodded a couple of times and looked up at me. "Nine a.m. tomorrow?"

I gave him the high sign and pulled out my cell phone to record the appointment. Spears thanked him and dropped the receiver.

"Guy's name is Ronald Couchell. *Captain* Ronald Couchell. He likes respect."

"Wouldn't have it any other way."

"Okay. Give," he said.

"The situation I can't talk about led me in a direction I didn't expect. I encountered a couple of kids, college students. They ostensibly got into a fight at a frat house kegger the night of the assault, maybe a half hour afterward. They both have scraped up knuckles, and both claim they punched a tree."

"Both of them?"

"What are the chances? So, I walked the route from the fieldhouse to the frat house four different ways before I came up here. You know. Four ways for four assailants. You told me they all took off in different directions."

"Yeah."

"Not one of the routes took more than fifteen minutes. It would have been possible to jump Hunt, scatter, and arrive back at the frat house easily before the fight took place."

"Kind of a stretch," Spears said. "Hope you didn't make me waste a favor for something that weak."

"Wait. One of the kids is a student in Hunt's forensic psych course. Smart kid. Ambitious. Black."

"Uh-oh," Spears said.

"He's also a jock. Baseball shortstop. I've heard Hunt ridicule him in the classroom. I interviewed him. He's grudging pretty hard against Hunt. Wouldn't mind showing him what the thick end of a baseball bat feels like."

"Gotta get in line for that these days."

"True enough. But hear me out. Sonny's going to tail the other kid. I confronted both kids in the student union earlier today, and they know I suspect them...you know, of this other matter. But, like I said, I think the two might be related, so I'm bringing you up to speed."

"What do you expect to find?"

"I'm betting Sonny will see the other kid, Mark Ballenger, meet up with one or two people yet unknown to us, who also have bruised and scabbed knuckles. They know I thought their story sucked, so they're going to have to coordinate a new one. I think they'll hook up as a group to try to figure a way out their mess. Sonny will see it, and we'll have all your suspects. If they pan out, your case gets solved, and maybe ours as well. At the very worst, you get your guys, and I can eliminate them from my equation."

Spears thought it over. "I don't know," he said.

"Oh, come on, Dexter. We have means, we have motive, we have opportunity, and a really shitty story about how their hands got bloodied. You could light an official fire under their butts. Interview them, badges, lights, maybe a uniformed backup. Tell them you got an anonymous tip and make them account for every second of their time the night Hunt was attacked. Make them nervous. Maybe, between us, they'll collapse and give us the whole story."

"Sounds like a dry hole to me," Spears said. "If they have multiple wits saying they were at this party the night Hunt was attacked, I got nothing."

I didn't have to be San Francisco's Most Noted Detective to recognize the kiss-off. Spears wasn't going to do anything. His—and the department's—blind spot regarding Hunt stood between them and justice. A story as old as guys wearing brass and tin. It was one of the reasons I left the force.

"I don't know why I'm trying to sell you," I said. "We already completed our transaction. I gave you what I got." I slid a sheet of paper with contact information for Mark Ballenger and Tony Richardson onto his desk. "You decide what to do with it. Thanks for calling Captain Couchell."

TWENTY-FOUR

I escorted Hunt to his place and took off for the night. Sonny had the Ballenger kid under surveillance, and the Celtic harp had been calling me for days, so I scooted down the coast to the Montara house to make some sawdust. I was at the point of rasping out the primary shape of the upper arch, an intensely satisfying activity strongly akin to sculpture. I clamped it in the bench vise between two strips of leather, and attacked it with rasps, files, and rifflers. It was a lot like the quote I'd once heard made by one of the great sculptors. *I carve away every piece that isn't a horse,* or something to that effect. I had a mental image of what I wanted the arch to look like, and I just kept grinding away at it until that vision emerged.

While gratifying, it was largely mindless activity. It cleared my head and gave me time to try to tie together all the divergent pieces of the Hunt case. I still couldn't figure out how the blonde, Amy Beth Popowicz fit in. Showing up on both ends of our investigation set off all sorts of red flags. I made a mental note to drop by the office in the morning and do a computer search on her. If you think Google is comprehensive, you should see the Batcave-level search engines detectives can access for an unsurprisingly exorbitant fee. It would be interesting to find out whether Amy Beth had enjoyed any previous brushes with the law. Sonny put it right. Coincidences suck. I don't trust them.

Even without Amy Beth in the equation, things looked screwy. With luck, the next morning I'd find out who wrote the blackmail note to Hunt. The electric buzzing in the back of my head was either a stroke, or a warning. Something about the whole blackmail situation was off. It took me a while, but finally it hit me.

What happened to the extortionists? It had been over a week since the assault, and not a word. They'd gone to great lengths to acquire incriminating pictures and generate an almost untraceable blackmail note. When Hunt didn't give in to their demands, they sent some toughs to bounce him around a little. If I were a blackmailer, what would I do next? The reasonable move was to reassert their demands, and maybe tack one or two more on just to be punitive.

But Hunt's blackmailers had gone dark. Why hadn't they gotten back in touch?

Being a natural cynic, it occurred to me they might have, and Hunt had kept it from me. Having hired two potentially frightening men as protectors might have emboldened him, made him feel invincible, so he just ignored the new demands the way you'd dodge a collection agency's phone calls.

Another possibility: Tony Richardson, Mark Ballenger and two other guys weren't the blackmailers. They kicked the shit out of Hunt at the direction of a third party, the real blackmailers. That's where Amy Beth Popowicz re-entered the story. She was in the pictures, and she was the ostensible reason for the fight at the frat house.

Bringing Amy Beth back into the story reminded me of Sandy Dennis, which was about three seconds before the lights went on.

Brandon Hunt told me he met Sandy Dennis in a bar, and she offered him mollies. Sandy reported that they met in a bar, but it was Hunt who had the drugs. I'd presumed Hunt was lying, and even accused him of it to his face.

Maybe he told the truth after all. Hunt is a well-known face around the college community. A lot of people hate him. Maybe someone decided to do something about it.

I started to pull the threads together in my head. Sandy Dennis was an Asian woman, who Hunt would typically despise unless it was to his benefit. She set her own honeypot trap for him in the bar. When he showed up, she sidled up to him. Maybe she talked to him about her work with Dr. Friedman, exactly the way she said. And then, she lured him back to her place with the promise of drug-enhanced carnal delights. They both agreed that Sandy offered to bring in a third player. What if she had always planned to? She picked out Amy Beth, who immediately jumped on the opportunity, euphemistically speaking. During the ensuing Twisterfest, Sandy or Amy Beth—or both—took incriminating photos. After Hunt left, they plotted the extortion.

And now we circled back to Mark Ballenger and Tony Richardson. When Hunt didn't knuckle under after receiving the blackmail note, Sandy and Amy Beth decided to increase the stakes. Amy Beth used her demonstrated powers of seduction to wrangle Mark Ballenger, Tony Richardson, and two players to be named later to put the hurt on him. They pulled their punches because dead men don't pay out, and because they really are just a bunch of college kids, not professional thugs.

Somebody in the group must be very good at planning details. That person realized the assailants might need an alibi for the evening, so they planned the loud public fight at the frat house. Amy Beth being right in the middle clinched it.

If I was right, I'd know as soon as the next morning. If either Sandy or Amy Beth picked up the paper from the printer in the security videos, I'd have them cold.

As I rasped away on the Celtic harp, I realized the tension in my shoulders had sloughed away, and I had begun to smile.

After she closed the gallery, Heidi drove down to join me. She brought a pizza. I didn't tell her I'd eaten some for lunch. People disappoint Heidi at their peril.

We selected the Iron and Wine channel on Pandora, and Heidi opened a bottle of wine. I preferred beer with pizza. Thankfully, a six-pack of Anchor Steam had taken up residence in my refrigerator. I grabbed a quick shower to shake off the sawdust, tossed on a cutoff sweatshirt and some shorts, and joined her on the couch.

"I don't know what smells better, the walnut or you after that shower," she said.

"I used that soap you gave me," I said. "Thought you'd like it."

"What's up with the fascist?"

"I think I solved it."

"Good for you. Solving a case always makes you nice and cuddly. Who done it?"

"I'll know for sure tomorrow." I gave her a brief outline, without divulging names.

"Kids today." She shook her head. "Who can figure them out? What will you do if you're right?"

"I have a couple of choices. I already gave two of the guys to Dexter Spears at SFPD, but I don't think he's going to follow up on it."

"He didn't believe you?"

"He's lazy and doesn't give two shits about Brandon Hunt. The case isn't a priority for anyone downtown. Spears probably hopes they'll kick his ass again."

"So...nothing?"

"Oh, there'll be something. What it is, is up to Hunt. He might want this handled *sub rosa*. I'm not a real cop. I can't arrest anyone. I can put the fear of God in them, though. If I'm right, and I should know tomorrow morning, Sonny and I will pay a visit to each of the little miscreants. We'll remind them what the penalties are for extortion and assault, and maybe make them piss their pants a little. Maybe we'll convince them they're being watched, and any false steps will mean a quick trip to the pokey."

She giggled a little. The wine was getting to her. "You think you're scary."

"No, but Sonny's a beast."

My telephone buzzed on the end table. Sonny.

"Speak of the devil," I told her, before answering. "What's up, partner?"

Sonny apparently called from outside. I could hear traffic noise in the background.

"It's going down," he said. "The Ballenger kid met up with Richardson about ten minutes ago, and they walked toward the stadium. They picked up two other guys near the fieldhouse, and they all got into a third car. I got the plate number. I think this is the meet you expected."

He read the license tag number, and I jotted it down.

"Keep an eye on them," I said. "Once they let Mark and Tony off, stay on their tail. Find out where they live."

"One more thing. I had to lay back pretty far, but I got a good look at the other two guys' hands with the binoculars."

"Yeah?"

"I couldn't tell for certain, but they looked pretty beat up."

"Maybe they've been punching trees. Get their names, and I'll let you shake them down," I said.

"Finest kind," he said.

TWENTY-FIVE

In the old days, I'd have dashed out the door to join Sonny the instant he called. Time and tide, as they say. Maybe I'm not as eager as I used to be. Sonny was new to the game, but he had twenty years of nefarious experience on which to draw. His training as an Army Ranger gave him the ability to disappear in an instant. If you were lucky, he didn't reappear. His time in the trenches with the dangly remnants of the San Francisco Mediterranean mob had taught him how to be tough enough, without losing control. I figured he could handle himself.

Beyond that, sooner or later the fledglings must leave the nest and fly on their own. I'd taught him how to exploit databases and mine public and private records. I'd taught him how to conduct a decent interview. I'd given him the tools and a few tips on how to use them. I could tell he was getting itchy for some action, though. We'd done a few stakeouts and pursuits together. It was time for him to solo.

For one night, I could relax and enjoy the privilege of sharing a pizza and some righteous music with a Teutonic goddess and forget about Brandon Hunt for a few hours.

Best laid plans.

I was just getting really friendly with Heidi around eleven, when my cell buzzed. Sonny again.

"When you're right..." he started.

"What's up?"

"I followed the car to an off-campus apartment complex. A real build and burn kind of place. Always amazes me how college students live—myself included, back in the day."

"A story as old as time," I said.

"Anyway, as I said, it's an apartment building, with exterior mailboxes. The four of them piled out of the car and into apartment One-G, building Thirty Six Hundred Two. I found the mailbox for One-G. Two names—Plyler and Dean. They stayed there maybe an hour, and then they hopped back into the car and peeled out of the parking lot. Want to guess where they went next?"

"Does it involve Amy Beth Popowicz?"

"Way to step on a guy's punchline," Sonny said. "I bow to your omniscience. Yeah. They parked in front of her dorm, and she climbed into the car with them. They're back at the apartment now."

"Give me the address again," I said. He read it off. I wrote on a pad on the nightstand. "Okay. Stay on them. Let me know if she stays the night, or they take her back to the dorm. If she's still there by four, head to the barn."

"Sounds like you need another conversation with Inspector Spears."

"Why bother?" I said. "He made his position clear this afternoon. We're working the extortion case, not the assault, even if we think they are related. I'll get back with Spears if we find something concrete. Guy has to do something for himself someday."

———————

My phone buzzed around four-fifteen. Sonny texted *'Headed home. You get first babysitter watch in a.m'.*

I drifted back to sleep; my phone alarm set for eight. It was Saturday, and Hunt had told me he planned to sleep in, so I could afford to miss the sunrise for once.

Instead of my alarm, my ringer went off at seven-forty-five. Brandon Hunt.

"What—" I started.

"They did it!" he shouted. "They released the fucking pictures!"

He was so loud, Heidi stirred next to me in the bed. I threw on a robe and headed for the living room, talking all the way.

"Hold up," I said. "Are you talking about *the* pictures?"

"And a few more."

"Where did they—"

"*Everywhere*, man! Fucking Snapchat. Reddit. Pornhub. Name a site. There's even fucking *video!* I am, like, so fucking fucked!"

"How'd you find out?" I said.

"Got a phone call about an hour ago. The college president. Needless to say, this was all the board needed to exercise the moral turpitude clause in my tenure contract. I'm out. They fucking canned me, Gold."

I could hear him begin to break down in tears.

"Are you at your apartment?"

"No. I have a place on the beach in Pacifica. Just a surf shack, really. Soon as I heard from the president, I took off. I'll be there in about ten minutes."

"Give me the address," I said. "I'm in Montara myself. I can be in Pacifica before you get there."

"Fuck off, Gold! You think I want to see your sorry face right now? You were supposed to *keep* this from happening."

"You hired Sonny and me to protect you. You're alive. Mission accomplished. If you recall, you withheld the blackmail from me. But if you're dissatisfied with our service, I can resign the case and refer you to another highly reputable agency in town. Sheldon Moon—"

"Resign the case?" he said. "You're *fired.*"

"Ends the same either way," I said. "I'll prepare your bill and send it along with the referral later today. Have a nice day, Doctor Hunt."

"Motherf—" was all I heard before I punched the call off. I called Sonny.

"The fuck, Eamon?" he mumbled on answering.

"Shut it down and sleep in," I said.

"What?"

"The blackmailers pulled the trigger. There are pictures of Hunt shagging coeds all over social media. The college fired him. He passed it down to us. The case is dead."

"Just like that?"

"What else are they gonna do? Beat him up again? The bad guys ran the clock out on us this time, partner. They took this one with a buzzer beater. It happens. We'll get them next time."

"But all that stuff we know about the four stooges and Blondie—"

"I have file cabinets full of stories like that," I said. "They'll trot on it. This time. If they keep it up, they'll screw around eventually and get caught. They usually do. So, tuck yourself in and grab some serious rack time. You've earned it."

"Thanks. Smell you later." He rang off.

I turned my phone to private, returned to the bedroom, and slipped back under the covers. Blackout curtains rendered the room almost inky. As my head settled into the pillow, Heidi rolled over.

"'S'up, lover?" she asked.

"Snow day," I said. "Don't have to go to school. We can sleep in."

"Ooooh," she said, almost a sigh. "And then pancakes?"

"You bet. Pancakes sound good."

"Bet your ass they do," she said. Seconds later, she snored lightly.

It took me a while to get to sleep. What I'd said to Sonny wasn't entirely true. Maybe a bunch of college kids didn't really run the clock out on us. It bothered me that I might have accelerated that clock by confronting Tony Richardson and Mark Ballenger in the food court. Their relative youth made me cocky. I had forgotten that the same youth meant they didn't think things through entirely and were more likely to act out of emotion. Fear, for instance.

By openly challenging them, it was possible I'd frightened them into pulling the pin on Hunt's entire life.

Just before I drifted off, I decided it was important for me to figure out how I felt about that.

TWENTY-SIX

I spent most of Saturday scraping and sanding the upper arch into a semifinished state and set about laminating three more flitches of walnut to form the lower arch. Heidi lounged on the sofa and watched Eddie Muller host some old noir flicks on TCM. We broke for dinner at the Chart House and took a walk north along the beach afterward to help our digestion.

"You're contemplative today," she said, holding my hand as the tips of the waves lapped at our bare feet. The water was like ice, but it felt strangely soothing.

"This Hunt stuff is bouncing around my head," I said.

"I thought you couldn't stand him."

"He's obnoxious and reprehensible, but he's my client."

"*Was* your client."

Which was true enough, since I'd sent his final bill via email earlier in the day. So far, he hadn't responded.

"See," I said, "there's this code among private cops. Once the guy is a client, all the personal stuff goes into cold storage. I had one job—to protect him. Instead, I might be responsible for his firing."

"You didn't screw coeds," she said. "What's happening to Hunt would have happened eventually with or without you. For all we know, those two kids in the food court might have been planning to attack him again when you showed up. You may have saved him from further injury."

"By having him tossed out on his ear?"

"That's on them," she said. "If they decided to dump the pictures on the Internet, that makes them the bad guys. You can't see the future. You can only do what you do. Speaking of which, what do you do next?"

"Hunt isn't going to like the bill I sent him, but it will cover my nut for several months. Something will turn up."

"It always does," she said.

"Yes," I said. "It always does."

———————

Sonny called me on Sunday morning. "Earleen and I are doing brunch in a couple of hours. Want to join us?"

I covered the phone and stuck my head into the shower, where Heidi was soaped up and getting ready to rinse. "Brunch with Sonny and Earleen? Around noon?"

She nodded and stuck her head under the water.

"Sure thing," I told Sonny. "Where?"

"The soul food place on Polk. Brenda's."

"Count us in."

"See you there."

Brenda's French Soul Food on Polk Street was a lot like Brennan's in New Orleans. Upscale Creole and low country fare with a French twist, usually served only after a half-hour wait on the sidewalk. Sonny and Earleen were already seated when Heidi and I arrived. They had already ordered a plate of crawfish beignets, half of which still remained in the middle of the table.

"How'd you get seated so quickly?" I asked as we took our seats across from them, and Heidi started in on the beignets.

"Friend of the family," Earleen said. "They always take me right in. Who wants mimosas?"

It took Earleen two mimosas—on top of the one she'd had in front of her when we arrived—to finally work up the courage to ask. By then, we had all ordered our entrees, which had just arrived at the table.

"So," she said tentatively, "about Brandon."

"No longer in his employ," I said.

"Yeah. Sonny told me. The whole campus is buzzing about his firing, and it's still just the weekend. Come Monday morning, yow."

"*Yow* about sums it up," I said. "I...uh...I guess you saw the pictures."

"Nothing I haven't seen before," Earleen said. "Figured I'd seen the last of that skinny white ass."

"I haven't seen them," Heidi said. Earleen pulled them up on her phone and handed it to her. After flipping through half a dozen, Heidi whistled. "Difficulty factor of three-point-two. Are those girls even legal?"

"The two in that picture are," I said. "What do you suppose will happen to his classes?"

"They're going online, with substitute professors. Gonna be a lot of disappointed little Hitler Youth, now that their Fuhrer isn't at the head of the class anymore."

I said, "I don't know. Most of the students I saw in his classes seemed to be there for the curiosity value."

"That's how indoctrination starts," Earleen said. "It's old corporate advertising psychology. First you grab their attention. They aren't listening, they aren't changing their minds. Fascist clowns like Brandon are how you get 'em under the big top. Then you bring out the lions. Soon as the students show up on Monday and find out Hunt isn't on the playbill, there'll be a run at the drop/add office. I'll put ten dollars on it."

"No takers," I said.

Earleen wrapped her arm around Sonny's arm and beamed. "Well, something good came out of it. Got a chance to finally hang with this guy."

Sonny looked a little sheepish. It was cute as hell.

A minute later, Earleen excused herself to visit the ladies'. Heidi, adhering to the Creed of All Women, went with her.

"They're talking about us, you know," Sonny said.

"Egotist," I said. "You cool with how things went down, partner?"

"I will be. I still don't think it's right those kids get a pass."

"Half of the criminal population gets a pass their entire lives," I said. "How many years did JuneBug spend in the slam? None. And he was, like, a hundred when you and he got shot, and he was already dying from cancer of the everything. By all rights, he should have died with his face in a rancid jail pillow. It's just the way things are."

"It'll catch up with them sooner or later," he said. "One way or the other. If they'll do it to Hunt, they'll do it to each other."

"Now you're learning."

My phone buzzed. I checked it. Hunt.

"Strange," I said, and took the call.

"This is Brandon—" he started.

"I know. What can I do for you?"

"You still in Montara?"

"I'm in the city. I'll be back down that way later this afternoon."

"You know when?"

"Why?" I asked.

Long silence. "I...I want to talk."

I muted the phone and said to Sonny, "He wants to talk."

"Billable hours, baby," Sonny said.

I unmuted the phone. "Five o'clock?"

"Yeah," he said. "Five's fine. I'm texting you my address."

We both rang off without saying goodbye.

TWENTY-SEVEN

When Hunt said he had a surfer shack on the beach in Pacifica, he wasn't far wrong. Coat-tailing on the tiny house binge, some entrepreneurial sort had erected a series of what appeared to be single-wide mobile homes with weather-resistant siding, narrow wrap-around decks, cinder-block foundations, tiny screened porches, and a couple of parking spaces each. They were arranged diagonally to the tide line to maximize the ocean view from inside. The sand was mere feet from the houses. They probably cost forty grand apiece to install and sold for half a million each. America. Is this a great country or what?

I dropped Heidi off at my Montara house so she could take her car back into the city and I waited for her to leave before I changed clothes for my visit with Brandon Hunt. I arrived at his unit exactly at five. He sat outside, nursing a beer at a concrete picnic table next to the parking lot and staring at the ocean. When I got out of the car, he pulled a dripping bottle from a cooler on the bench next to him and held it up to me. It wasn't a brand I'd have picked for myself, but I'm not particular.

I twisted the cap and took a sip. It wasn't as bad as I expected. Hunt reached inside his jacket and pulled out an envelope, which he slid across the table to me.

"Your check," he said.

I slipped the envelope into the inside pocket of my windbreaker, and I waited. Something in his voice suggested Hunt hadn't summoned me just to hand over a check.

"It's all there," he said.

"I don't doubt it. Once you've seen Sonny, you wouldn't dare short us."

He chuckled. "No. I wouldn't. Surprised your shadow isn't here with you."

"Yeah," I said. "Okay, this is fun, but I have stuff to—"

"Wait!" he said. "I'm sorry."

"I don't think so."

"Well, I am."

"You want an audience, and I'm the only guy left who will listen to you."

He laughed out loud this time.

"That's *all* they want, Gold!" He held up his cellphone. "Call after call. All weekend. Fox News. Newsmax. OAN, The Daily Stormer. Every whacko conspiracy-peddling video tabloid there is. Bill Maher. *Bill fucking Maher.* They all want me. People have been throwing money at me all day. Big numbers. Gag an elephant numbers."

"And, the universe again wobbles out of balance," I said.

"Tell me about it," he sighed.

I tried to give him one of those Sonny Malehala eyebrow things. He threw up his hands and stood, facing the ocean.

"I'm not going to take it! For real? You think that's what I want? You know who they're buying? They want the social heresy-shouting guy who everyone's seen gagging some coed with his dick on PornHub. I'm the Freak of the Week, man. Nobody is ever going to take me seriously again. I'll never see the inside of another classroom."

"Is there a downside to all this?"

He whirled back around. "Always with the jokes."

"Who's joking?"

He opened another beer. "What happened, man? How did it get to this point? Why?"

"Do you have no idea at all how your words affect other people?" I asked. "They have power. You have no use for any person of color until you have a specific use for them. The hypocrisy boggles the mind. Outing you as a cradle-robbing horndog was probably the goal all along."

"What about the assault?"

"I'm pretty sure your student Tony Richardson was part of it, along with another student named Mark Ballenger and two others named Plyler and Dean."

"Richardson. I'll flunk his ass..." He took another swig from the bottle.

"You aren't in that position anymore. For what it's worth, I gave Richardson and Ballenger to Inspector Spears for the assault. He knows their names. If he follows up, it will lead to the extortion."

"It'll never happen," Hunt said.

"You're probably right."

He cradled his head on his crossed arms on the concrete tabletop and stared off at the ocean.

"So, this is how it ends," he said.

"It's how something else begins," I said. "I have a good friend who's a porn producer in Marin County. If you want to go into show biz, I can hook you up."

"Fuck you, man," he said, and sat back up to take another chug from the rapidly depleting bottle. "Were you around during the old NASA Mercury days?"

"Before my time," I said.

"Me too. I watched a movie about the program the other night. It was highly fictionalized. They had a scene just before a launch, with the astronaut strapped into his seat, lying on his back, staring at the sky through the porthole. Something was wrong, and the countdown was on hold. Finally, sick and tired of waiting, the astronaut demanded they launch. He said, *'C'mon, boys! Punch that button! I can't wait to get to the wild black yonder!'.*"

He dropped another empty into the cooler and started in on a freshie.

"The black yonder," he slurred. "I reckon we're all headed in that direction, sooner or later. In the last day and a half, I've felt it looming even closer. You ever think about death, Gold?"

"Who doesn't?"

"Right. But nobody admits it. From the time we're old enough to conceive of a future, we know there will come a point when we aren't in it. You might find this funny, given my supposedly radical right leanings, but I'm an atheist. My end of the political spectrum believes it has coopted religion. Me? I know it's all malarkey intended to control the masses. So, I look on the other side of the grass, and I don't see salvation. You know what I see?"

"The black yonder?"

"Damn skippy. Cold and dark and unseeing and unfeeling and unthinking until the heat death of the universe. Used to scare the shit out of me when I was a kid. Twelve years old, and I'm damn near wetting the bed because of panic attacks over the freshly acquired knowledge that I was in a dead-end existence. There was an unavoidable and inevitable end of the line waiting out there. I was speeding toward it, and I had no brakes. Funny thing. Older I get, the less I fear it. Age and experience make cynics of us all. We see the repetition of history and the folly of humans, and we recognize the truth. Humans are a tragic mistake. We infest this planet. We are not enveloped in grace. Worse, we understand after a few decades that we are surfing the entropic wave. Not only will nothing ever get better. With time, it will become only more chaotic. Heisenberg and all that. Who wants to hang around for humanity's curtain call?"

"You're lecturing," I said.

"It's my thing. You got a gun on you?"

"I don't typically arm myself to pick up a check."

"You ever kill anyone?"

I thought about four moldering bodies in a Napa vineyard. I thought about Frank Raymond standing in a pool of light in an Alameda industrial park. I thought about a hulking computer nerd sitting on an office floor clawing at the hole in his chest. I thought about all the nights of sleep they'd cost me. In each case, it had been them or me, and it was far better that they died and I lived. They might disagree, but they were already in the depths of the black yonder and could no longer plead their cases.

"Shit like this keeps me awake at night," I said.

"That's a chickenshit answer, Gold."

"I've killed people. And that's all I care to say about it."

"So hooked on your hero ethos and your fucking code that you can't face up to the image of yourself as a killer?"

His check was in my pocket, and I'd had about all I could stand of his toxic bullshit. Even in utter defeat and disgrace, Brandon Hunt did and said whatever he could think of to make himself feel superior. Even at the nadir of his life, he was an inveterate bully.

"Delete my number from your phone," I said. "Take the TV jobs. I have a feeling you'll find kindred souls there. Thanks for the check. Gotta jet."

I walked toward my car. Hunt yelled after me.

"Hey, Killer! If I make a million bucks, can I hire you again to take down the little shits who did this to me?"

I ignored him and kept walking.

TWENTY-EIGHT

Until it abruptly ends, life goes on. A few weeks blew by. As Sonny said, the beast must be fed, so I put Brandon Hunt in the rearview and moved on to the next case.

The air was crisp with a slight tinge of leaf smoke as Heidi and I crossed the Golden Gate into Marin County. It was October, and the sky spanned over us like a transparent blue globe, not a cloud in sight.

We had taken Heidi's Miata. She had permitted me to drive, which was kind of a treat after slogging around my eight-year-old boring forgettable stakeout-mobile. She sat in the passenger seat, her hair pulled back in a blonde French braid and covered with a silk Hermes scarf, looking like Tippi Hedren driving across to Bodega Bay, only more so. I had dressed down for the occasion, jeans and a long-sleeved blue oxford cloth shirt, with a light hounds-tooth tweed jacket and loafers.

Heidi leaned her head back and smiled as she kneaded my thigh. It was okay. She was along for a pleasure ride.

I was working.

"So where is this place?" she asked.

"Tiburon."

"Oh, goody. I like Tiburon. I haven't been to Tiburon in ages."

"When was the last time you were in Tiburon?"

"Damned if I can recall. What's the story there?"

"I don't know. A guy called me yesterday, said he wanted to hire me. I suggested that he come to my office. He insisted on meeting at his club in Tiburon. That's about all I know."

"He didn't say why?"

"Not a word."

"How did he sound?" she asked, as her hand inched up my thigh. I could feel involuntary muscles contract around my boy stuff.

"Like a man with a lot on his mind," I said.

Alan Standish greeted us in the lobby at the Pampas Polo Club in Tiburon. The building looked and felt new on the inside, but the exterior had been carefully contrived to resemble an Argentine *estancia*, with pink stucco walls and vaulted windows covered with wrought-iron grates. The grounds were lush with weeping willows, and gently arched bridges spanning quiet streams that flowed between perfectly groomed hills. The place looked like a well-tended cemetery.

Standish was tall and lean, with a tan almost too perfect for nature. He had Robert Redford hair, wisps of which fell across his brow, making him look much more boyish than his age deserved. His teeth were like bleached marble tombstones. He wore a white silk shirt and tan jodhpurs, with gleaming knee-high black boots.

"Don't look now, but someone stole your pith helmet," I said.

He smiled, just a bit.

"I was practicing this morning. Polo. Do you play?"

"No."

"You seem athletic enough."

"Sure, but jodhpurs make my butt look huge."

I introduced Heidi to Standish. He took her hand, and I noted that his eyes bounced from her face to her bosom and back again.

The cad.

"Your partner?" he asked, looking at me but still grasping her hand.

"Of a sort. You have a bar somewhere?"

"Of course."

"Would they allow Ms. Fluhr to sit there and drink while we talk?"

"I think they would be delighted," he said.

After we deposited Heidi in the bar with a pitcher of margaritas and my Amex card, Standish escorted me to his office. It was suitably impressive, with lots of walnut and red leather, and shelves full of impressive books that would probably crackle like live electrical wires if I dared to open the covers.

"Nice place," I said, as I took a seat on the loveseat.

"Thank you."

"My office is a lot like this."

Standish crossed the office to a cabinet built into the bookcase and opened it to reveal a bar.

"What's your pleasure?"

"I don't suppose you have a Scrimshaw Pilsner in there anywhere."

Standish poured a short glass of something brown from a decanter.

"Would Anchor Steam do?" he asked.

"Just this once."

Standish retrieved a bottle of Anchor from the refrigerator below the bar and poured it into a schooner glass.

"Your Ms. Fluhr is enchanting," she said, as he handed me the glass.

"She is a Nordic goddess," I said.

"But she isn't with your office."

"No. She's with my other life."

"Do you discuss your business with her?"

Standish seemed a little nervous.

"Sometimes," I said. "But I always change the names to protect the innocent."

"The, ah, innocent. Yes. You come highly recommended, Mr. Gold."

I didn't answer. Answering might have seemed immodest.

"I'm sure, in your profession, you run across a great many hapless individuals."

I nodded, mostly to keep him talking.

"My situation is embarrassing. Do you handle divorce work?"

"Sure. Half my business involves tailing errant or misbehaving spouses."

He stood and walked over to his desk, where he picked up a framed photograph. He handed it to me. The frame was filigreed pewter, cool and slightly oily. The woman in the picture was radiant.

"My wife," he said. "Isabel. We've been married for twenty-four years. The first two decades were…well, wonderful. Soon after our twentieth anniversary, she became restless."

"Restless," I said.

"Irritable. She found fault in the most meaningless things. She squabbled over trivial matters. At first, I thought it must have something to do with menopause. She was the right age. I mentioned it to her once. The idea seemed to enrage her."

"How old is your wife, Mr. Standish?"

"Fifty-three."

"Still in the flower of youth these days. Fifty is the new thirty. A woman her age might not appreciate having her feelings written off as hormonal storms."

"No. There are other behaviors though. Telephone calls in the night. Unexplained absences. At times, I try to reach her through her cell phone, and it is turned off."

"What do you suspect?" I asked, though I already knew the answer.

"I believe she is having an affair."

166

I took a long sip of the Anchor Steam, and allowed it to flow down my throat, as I prepared my standard spiel for cuckolded husbands.

"Mr. Standish, I will be happy to tail your wife. If she is having an affair, I'll find out, and I'll find out who the other guy is. I'll get you pictures. If you'd prefer, I can get you video. I can provide you with enough evidence to assure an uncontested divorce."

He nervously raised his glass and drank some of the brown stuff. He didn't seem to enjoy it.

"However," I continued. "I should advise you of something before taking this case. This kind of investigation is a one-way street. There's no u-turn. Right now, all you have are suspicions. Lots of people have midlife flings and settle back into their marriages. What you don't know can't hurt you. After I give you the hard evidence, though—and I can tell you this from experience—you are never going to see Isabel the same way again. If you are absolutely certain you want a divorce, then I'll get you the goods. If there is a shadow of a doubt, however, I'd advise holding off. You might feel differently in a week or so."

"You make a compelling argument," Standish said. "However, there is more. I don't work here. I have this office because I am president of the polo club. I'm an attorney, by trade. My office is in the city. Do you know much about polo, Mr. Gold?"

"Not a lot."

"It is a regal sport. It is also extremely competitive. This may look like a country club, and in many ways it is.

However, it is also the headquarters for a highly-regarded professional sports team."

"Professional polo."

"Yes. And, as president of the Pampas Club, I am also the nominal president of our polo team."

"Heavy hangs the head," I said.

"You have no idea. Like a great many landed polo clubs around the country, we recruit the top talent to play for us. We offer these individuals incentives and significant salaries."

"How significant?"

"For riding a horse and batting a ball around a field? Very significant. Not as much as they pay basketball or football players, but a lot. A great number of the better polo riders are from other countries, most of them in South America."

"Argentina, for instance," I said, waving my hand around.

"Yes. The Pampas Polo Club is not named by accident."

"What does this have to do with your wife?"

He took another sip. He tried to make it look dashing. I saw it for what it was—a stall. He reached into his desk drawer, extracted a picture, and handed it to me. Blond fellow. Good looking, to the extent a confident heterosexual man can judge. Athletic.

"Gavrillo Weber." He pronounced the last name *Vayber.*

"Sounds German."

"He looks German, too. Tall, lean, blond, blue-eyed, the whole stereotype. He doesn't talk about it much, but I suspect his grandparents escaped to Argentina from Germany toward the end of World War Two."

"Nazis?"

Standish shrugged. "Who knows? Gavrillo is our club's star rider. I brought him here from South America on a work visa and gave him a job with my firm. Gavrillo Weber has gone missing," he said. "He's been off the chart for about a week. About two days after he first failed to show up for work at the law firm, I noticed some discrepancies in one of the client accounts. I double-checked it, but still couldn't determine where about ten thousand dollars had gone. So, I ran a check of several other accounts, and they seemed to have been raided also, all for small percentages of their gross balance. Nobody's account was wiped out, but a lot of them had been plundered."

"You think Weber skimmed your client accounts, and then took off."

"That's exactly what I think, Mr. Gold. Now, here's the connection. I can't prove it, but I believe the man my wife is screwing is Gavrillo Weber. Further, I think she knows where he is. You follow her, I think you'll find him. I don't suppose I need to tell you what could happen if it were to come out that someone had taken money from my firm's client accounts."

"You'd be disbarred."

"Hell, I'd probably be imprisoned. I quietly replaced the missing money with my own, and issued orders that Weber isn't to be allowed back in the office. I want as much of that money back, though, as I can get. I want you to find Weber, get my money back, and also prove that he's been shagging my wife, so that I can divorce her."

"Sounds like fun," I said.

TWENTY-NINE

"So, what's the job?" Heidi asked as we pulled into The Pelican Inn parking lot outside the entrance to Muir Woods. Heidi had a hankering for British pub food, though for the life of me I couldn't figure out why. I'm a good sport, though, so I played along.

"Standard stuff. Divorce and embezzlement."

"A double-header," she said.

We were seated, and I looked over the menu.

"Are you taking it?" she asked, as she unfolded her napkin.

"Think I'll hand it over to Sonny," I said. "His first solo case."

"Not interesting enough?"

"He has to fly sometime. I've handled dozens of these cases. I'll stay in the background and offer sage timely advice."

"From the safety of your wood shop, I suppose," she said.

I'd completed construction on the Celtic harp in a flurry of activity after my last meeting with Brandon Hunt. I was letting it age and relax a little before applying the finish. While waiting, I had moved on to a Benedetto-style archtop guitar a jazz musician friend of mine in the city had requested. Thanks to Hunt, and to Barbara Ledford's generous cut of her new software, I was bucks-up and didn't have to scat around town scaring up work.

"The job comes in ebbs and flows," I said. "I'm enjoying a little vacation."

"You don't seem to be enjoying anything these days," she said. "Vacating, yes. Loving it, not so much. What's eating you, Sugar? You've had cases go south before."

"No use arguing, I suppose. I can't get the Hunt case off my mind. I've been retracing my steps, and I keep coming to the same solution. I got cocky and tried to push around a couple of already scared kids. If I'd held back until Sonny finished his stakeout on them, we could have handed the entire package over to Dexter Spears with a clear conscience, regardless of what he did about them. Instead, one blunder and Hunt's entire life was torpedoed."

"Which never would have happened had he kept away from women students," Heidi argued. "You protected a very bad man, Eamon. I don't see that there was a way to win. Best you could hope for was a big paycheck, because either way you were going to feel like shit when the job was done."

My phone buzzed. The display read *B. Hunt*.

"I told you to delete my number," I said immediately upon answering.

"I'm lonely," Hunt said. He sounded like he was calling from the hold of the HMS Crazytown.

"I'll text you the number for the Animal Shelter. Adopt a dog."

"I want you," he said, his voice dripping with desperation. "I can't talk to anyone else."

"Our business relationship is over," I said. "Don't confuse me with one of your friends."

"That's just it. I don't have any friends. I took your advice and accepted a job with one of the twenty-four hour cable news operations. I'm not proud of it. I needed the money. I got it, too. So much money—"

"Then you can afford to pay a shrink. He'll listen to you all day long."

"You don't understand. I need to talk to someone who isn't just a sycophant or a hanger-on or in it for the bucks. I need someone I can trust to give it to me straight. Otherwise, I'm gonna drown in this media circus."

"Sucks to be you. Kinda sucks to talk to you too. I'm hanging up now."

"I confronted her," he continued.

"Who?"

"Sandy. Sandy Dennis. I went to her house, and I demanded that she tell me everything."

"And what happened after she threatened to call the cops?"

"You're right. It was impulsive. She denied everything. But I could see the guilt in her eyes. She knows I'm onto her."

"If you think you're in danger, call nine-one-one. You want protection, call Sheldon Moon. I'm texting his number now."

"I want you, dammit!"

"I'm not available. Heidi was right. There's no winning with you. Get help, Brandon. I mean that."

I ended the call, put my phone on private, and returned to the restaurant.

THIRTY

I slid the first picture across the desktop to Sonny.

"Her name's Isabel Standish. All her particulars are on the sheet stapled there. Address, DOB, car tags, phone number, etc."

"She's some plastic surgeon's long-term project," Sonny said. "An expensive one, too. This isn't some fly-by-night Earl Scheib job. This is high-end Los Angeles surgeons-to-the-stars level work. Bet she had a boob job and ass implants as well."

"Isabel Standish is Quarry Number One," I said. "Her husband, Alan, is an attorney here in the city, but he runs a polo club in Tiburon. An old story. She got the twenty-year itch and found someone to scratch it. Alan's highly disappointed, and has decided to move on, marriage-wise. It's a simple divorce surveillance, with a twist. I figured it's time you handled your first case."

He grinned like a kid who'd just been promoted to first string. "Thanks, Eamon. I won't let you down. But you said Isabel is Quarry Number One. And there's a twist?"

I slid the other picture across the desk. "Quarry Number Two. Gavrillo Weber. Argentinian polo ace and possible embezzler. His particulars are stapled to the back. Alan

Standish brought him to the states to play and gave him a job at his law firm. Weber has vanished, along with the skim from several of Standish's client accounts."

"Mr. Standish has a lot of problems on his plate," Sonny observed.

"He's chosen to shuffle two of them onto ours."

"I suppose the connection between Isabel and Gavrillo runs deeper than their relation to Alan Standish."

"Standish suspects Weber is the man Isabel is banging."

"Does he have any evidence?"

"Nothing material. That's where you come in. It's a simple tail job. Follow Isabel everywhere she goes, until she meets up with her paramour. We get bonus points if it's Weber, because Standish wants us to bring him back so he can make an example of the boy."

"Which means—?"

"He wants the kid deported, with prejudice. Standish implied there might be a substantial bonus if Weber resisted and got roughed up a little."

"Which we would never do," Sonny said.

"I never say never. There's only so much we can do. So far, I've been able to avoid being hired muscle, and I know you've had far too much of that life. We can persuade Weber to come back, but if he refuses…" I shrugged my shoulders.

"What if he resists?"

"We don't instigate, but we don't back down either. If he gets huffy, we're within our rights to chill him out. Isabel is our priority. Follow her and get the goods for Standish's divorce lawyer. If it leads us to Weber, we're done. If it doesn't, we can look for Weber another day."

Sonny and I both looked at the door when we heard steps on the stairs. One person. Sounded heavyset. A shadow appeared in the glass of my office door. My office is on the second floor of a mixed use building on Jefferson Street near Hyde Pier. It backs up to the bay. There's no elevator. To reach my office, you take a flight of sixteen steps from the sidewalk. I'm the only office at the end of the steps, so footfalls on the treads are my early warning system. The door swung open, and Detective Crymes of the Pacifica Police Department stepped inside.

He was tall but portly, just short of Falstaffian proportions. He wore an overcoat and a hat, because it had been raining in the city since dawn. His hair was longish and graying, hanging wetly over a slack, jowly face marked by the saddest eyes in the western hemisphere.

"Detective!" I said, as he closed the door behind him.

"Gold," he returned. It was about as cordial as we get.

Crymes took the seat next to Sonny. They looked each other over.

"You worked for JuneBug," Crymes said. Sonny stiffened a little. It had been almost a year, but he still didn't like his former boss referred to by his street name. He gathered himself and extended his hand.

"Sonny Malehala. I work for Eamon."

"There are two of you now?" Crymes moaned. "*Ay, caramba.*"

"What can I do for you?" I asked.

Crymes scratched at his chin and gave me the lie-detector look. "For starters, you can tell me how your phone number wound up in the cellphone directory of a dead man."

THIRTY-ONE

Strangely enough, it wasn't the first time I'd been asked that question. I had to hand it to Crymes, though. He knew how to pull a shocker.

I knew what he was doing, of course. There is nothing more acute than the perceptual powers of a man with twenty years in carrying a gun and a gold shield. He knows every tell in the book. Even if there's no way a court would ever accept it as evidence, there is no such thing as lying to such a man.

"You got me," I said. "I killed Cock Robin with my bow and arrow."

"What about Brandon Hunt?"

Sonny and I both looked at one another. The surprise on both our faces obviously convinced Crymes of our innocence.

"Okay," I said. "You have our attention."

"How do you know Hunt?" Crymes asked.

"He was a client. He terminated our services several weeks ago."

"What were you doing for him?"

"Mostly bodyguard stuff. You know the guy?"

"I've heard of him," Crymes said. His tone made his distaste clear.

"Then you might have heard he got a major beatdown a month ago. He was afraid they might do it again. You're saying he's dead?"

"Let's do things this way," Crymes said. "First you'll answer my questions, and then maybe I'll answer yours."

"Okay. Hunt approached me about five weeks ago, several days after he was attacked. Dexter Spears at SFPD pulled the case, and it was active, so we couldn't investigate the assault itself. Hunt hired Sonny and me to keep an eye on him and discourage any would-be thugs from gaining access."

"How'd that work out?"

"Last time I saw him, he was breathing and healthy. That was after he terminated our services."

"Why'd he do that?"

"He was fired from the university. Pictures of him having sex with coeds were leaked onto the Internet. Someone sent them to the college president. They revoked his tenure and sent him packing. He needed to trim his expenses. I saw him a day or so later, at his place in Pacifica. He settled his bill."

"And you didn't hear from him again."

"Just a telephone call. Yesterday."

"What time?"

"Early afternoon. Hold on."

I checked the call log on my cell phone.

"He called me at one-thirty-seven yesterday afternoon. The conversation lasted about two minutes. Maybe a little more."

"Where were you when he called?"

"At the Pelican Inn, across the bridge."

"You got a witness?"

"Heidi Fluhr. We had lunch together. I have the time-stamped credit card receipt."

"What did you and Hunt discuss yesterday?" Crymes asked.

"He sounded drunk. Said he wanted to talk. Said he couldn't trust anyone else."

"Now, that's sad. Did he sound threatened?"

"No. Doesn't mean he wasn't, though. In the course of my employ, Sonny and I identified a few possible names in the assault. I can give them to you if you'd like."

"Names of his attackers?" Crymes' eyebrows raised.

"Sure. Dexter Spears at SFPD has them too. Tony Richardson and Mark Ballenger. Two other kids named Plyler and Dean might be involved too, but Hunt fired us before we could find out much more about them."

"I thought it was an open SFPD case."

"That's why I shared what I found with Spears. So, Hunt's dead?"

"As of approximately four o'clock yesterday afternoon. About two and a half hours after you talked to him."

"I was with Heidi all afternoon."

"Nothing like a blonde alibi," Crymes said.

"So, how'd he die? He sounded distraught over the phone. Did he kill himself?"

"Hard to tell. He missed a TV interview this morning, and the producer was worried. Asked the Pacifica PD to do a safety check."

"Kind of a leap," Sonny said.

"Apparently Gold wasn't the only person he talked with yesterday. When the producer called to firm up the interview time, Hunt's tone bothered him. He was rambling. Didn't make a lot of sense. Producer figured he was just drunk or high and wrote it off until Hunt didn't phone in for the interview. A uniformed officer dropped by his place on the beach, and found him lying on the living room floor, naked and trussed up like a Thanksgiving turkey with a ball gag in his mouth and a plastic dry cleaning bag over his head."

"Ball gag makes me think more of a suckling pig," I said to Sonny.

"You're a sick man," Crymes said. "You don't sound surprised about the condition in which he was discovered."

"Sonny and I spent almost a week shadowing Hunt day and night. Well, mostly day, but after that small amount of time we can say with assurance that Hunt was the quintessential queer duck. You could tell me he was discovered hanging upside down from a standpipe in Alcatraz while wearing a tutu and a Viking helmet, super-glued to a dead goat, and I'd be unsurprised. That he's dead, though— well, I didn't see that one coming."

"I'm sure you've seen the pictures of him on the Internet in the last month," Sonny said. "Guy had some serious kink mojo."

"We think he was posed," Crymes said. "The medical examiner at the scene determined TOD by liver temp, but there were signs that suggested he didn't die by asphyxiation. Apparently, he was posed some while after death, according to the livor mortis. They're running a tox screen, but you know how long that'll take to come back. We might not know what killed him for weeks unless the autopsy finds significant trauma."

"Bruises, scratches, skin under the nails?" I asked.

"Still in process, but there was no outward sign of injury or a struggle."

"So why pose him?" Sonny asked.

"Maximum humiliation," I answered. "Maybe the last thing he heard was someone telling him the ridiculous position in which he'd be discovered, and then they did it. Revenge shit."

"That's cold," Sonny said.

"Gotta hate someone a lot to go to that kind of trouble," Crymes said. "You think one of those kids you ran across could do it?"

"Richardson could," I said. "He hated Hunt's guts. He's bright, but I don't know if he's creative enough to pull off something like the posing."

"Anyone else?"

I laughed.

"What's funny?" Crymes asked.

"About six months ago, a political action group assembled a petition that was sent to the university board, demanding Hunt's removal from the faculty. Waste of time, of course, since the board was hogtied due to the court order. They put it up for a voice vote and rejected the petition. In the next week, the board received over forty thousand emails calling them Nazi sympathizers and racist enablers. Some of the emails contained veiled threats."

I wasn't making Crymes' day, but I had a feeling nothing much would after the way it began.

"Forty thousand," I said. "Those are your suspects, Detective. Good luck."

———————

Satisfied that we weren't involved in the Brandon Hunt murder, Crymes left several minutes later. Sonny took off shortly after, to begin his surveillance of Isabel Standish. I didn't expect to see him much over the next several days unless he got really lucky. This was one time bad luck would be welcome. Bad luck meant more billable hours.

I'm not sure why I'd held information back from Detective Crymes. We've run up against each other many times in the past and had a grudging mutual respect. I could generally count on him to do the right thing. Even so, I hadn't told him about the blackmail I thought might be behind the assault.

Perhaps it was because I wasn't completely convinced of a connection myself. Coincidences suck, but they sometimes happen. Tony Richardson and Mark Ballenger had a troubled relationship that preceded the fight on the night of Hunt's attack. I hadn't heard squat from Dexter Spears since giving the kids to him, which meant either they didn't play out, or Spears round-filed the names and went back to kissing City Hall asses.

As for Amy Beth Popowicz—yeah, it was suspicious that she showed up on both sides of the investigation, but we already knew she got around. Again, a suspicious coincidence, but perhaps no more than that.

Maybe my cobbled hypothesis connecting the blackmail to the assault was right. Maybe it wasn't.

In the end, I concluded it was an honor thing. Hunt had made it clear I couldn't go to the police with the blackmail. After the pictures were released, he had a month to make a complaint before he died. If he did, Crymes would find out. I suspected Hunt kept the extortion to himself, even after the pictures were released. He might be dead, but my promise of discreet investigations remained in place. I didn't tell Crymes about the blackmailers because I owed Hunt the confidentiality he paid for.

On the other hand, he had asked me to look into it as part of my employment. I'd dropped the inquiry as soon as Hunt pulled the plug. I poked around on my computer keyboard and brought Hunt's file up for a refresher.

Perhaps it was time to finish the job.

THIRTY-TWO

Alan Standish might have maintained a thriving law practice
in downtown San Francisco, but his home was across the
Golden Gate Bridge in Mill Valley. Probably kept him closer
to his beloved polo ponies in Tiburon. It wasn't a gated
neighborhood, but it also wasn't the sort of place that took
kindly to tough guys sitting around in cars for hours on end.

Unless the Standishes were into some kinky stuff, it was
unlikely Isabel would cheat while she was at home, so it
wasn't necessary for Sonny to hang out at the end of their
driveway with a parabolic mic and a telephoto lens. He took
up position just outside the exit to the neighborhood in a
small strip shopping center. Standish had one of those
Bluetooth doorbells that recorded whenever someone
entered or left the house, so he was notified on his phone
when Isabel took off. He'd alert Sonny, who'd wait for her
car to arrive at the exit, at which point he took up the chase.

Acting as a bodyguard for a mob boss, Sonny had become
accustomed to standing or sitting in one place for hours on
end, always at the ready. Like a baseball outfielder, he might
have appeared to be relaxed and perhaps even a little
lackadaisical, but in fact he was constantly calculating. If

Isabel turned right, how would he get out of the parking lot in time to tail her? If she turned left, how far back should he stay and how many cars should he keep between them?

The secret to a good stakeout was to not become famous. For a guy Sonny's size, being unobtrusive can be a bit of a chore. Instead, he rolled down the car window, hung an arm out, and tried to look like he was waiting on a shopper. Just another henpecked—if somewhat economy sized—husband dragged from the house on a perfectly good afternoon when he'd much rather be taking a nap.

He pulled up a classical station on the satellite radio, and watched the exit to the Standishes' neighborhood intently, just in case the doorbell malfunctioned.

Sonny thought about a lot of things during a stakeout. There was plenty of time to think. The last month had been something of a whirlwind. Sonny reminded himself to thank his boss for the introduction to Earleen Marley, and for not-so-covertly setting them up. While they had not reached the same level of unorthodox commitment as Eamon and Heidi, he and Earleen had spent a gracious portion of their time since the Brandon Hunt case together. Earleen would call with tickets to a new museum opening. Sonny showed Earleen how much fun an afternoon at a Forty-Niners game could be and took her to an expensive dinner that night in apology. It seemed, every several days, one or the other found themselves with a spare ticket to one thing or another.

And then there was the hooking up. That happened early, like the first night they went out. It was sweet and delicious. Sonny had spent his entire career as either a soldier or a mob bodyguard, but his college training was in English literature, and he considered the time he spent after hours with Earleen to be inspired by the works of D.H. Lawrence by way of Larry Flynt. His work life, for the most part, had precluded relationships that lasted much longer than the bills placed on the dresser. He'd had his share of women, many of them exceptionally talented, but he wasn't prepared for the inventive delights Earleen conjured.

Sonny had spent his entire life alone, but he could see the advantages of having someone around who knew more about you than your hotel room number. The last month had been an unaccustomed pleasure. He thought he could grow to like it.

Alan Standish had provided several pictures of his wife. Sonny pulled them from his jacket pocket and studied them. The evidence of multiple tours under the knife were unmistakable, but he could tell the bones beneath the skin were excellent. The surgeons had been given great material. Perhaps out of spite, Standish had slipped a picture of Isabel posing in a microscopic bikini on Waikiki Beach into the deck. Sonny could make out the form of Diamond Head in the distant background. A connoisseur of the feminine form, he could also discern the telltale signs of breast enhancement.

Five points off for Isabel, Sonny mused. Closing in on fifty himself, he had learned to appreciate the beauty of an unimproved partner such as Earleen, whom had allowed herself to embrace the heady middle of life gracefully. He had guessed wrong about Isabel's booty however, which appeared to be stock and pristine. So, five points added back for her resistance to wretched excess. Her legs were what caught his attention, though. They were amazing legs. Cyd Charisse legs. The kind of legs Juliet Prowse used to fling toward the ceiling. Flipping through the pictures, it was obvious she knew they were great, as she showed them off at every opportunity. You work to your strengths.

It occurred to him that it might be inappropriate to leer at the photo of his client's wife. On the other hand, it helped him try to get into the head of both Isabel and her lover. She was in her fifties, but even so, if she was cheating her paramour was obviously a man of refined taste. That revelation tinkled the warning bells inside Sonny's head.

Standish had suggested that his wife's presumed philandering and the disappearance of his embezzling prize polo rider were related. According to the information Standish provided, Gavrillo Weber was only in his middle twenties. While May-October romances between youths and women of a certain vintage were not unknown—and were in fact, in some quarters, fashionable—he had a hard time imagining Isabel being interested in anything more from Weber than what he could provide in the sack. The info he had on Isabel suggested she was accustomed to the better things, and she was cultured and erudite. Sonny wondered what she could possibly have to discuss with the young man outside the bedroom.

If Isabel was stepping out, Sonny had a feeling, when he finally caught her in the act, her partner wouldn't be Gavrillo Weber.

His phone buzzed. A message from Standish. Isabel was headed out.

Sonny started the car, moved toward the parking lot exit, and waited for Isabel's Mercedes to appear.

She turned right, toward the bridge. Sonny fell in behind her, about ten car lengths back. He allowed a couple of flashy convertibles to separate him from her. As he had been taught, he used a plain-jane grocery-getter for the stakeout, a six-year-old Kia midsize. It had all the charisma of a pimple and the horsepower of a lawnmower, but high-speed chases were kind of rare in the private cop business. His beige suburban surrender car served a different purpose. It was practically invisible, especially compared to the sports cars ahead of him.

Sonny figured he would be perfectly fine if she didn't go directly downtown. One problem with trying to do a one-man tail—in the city parking is a bear. If she headed into the city for a shopping spree, he could easily lose her by the time he found a space for himself.

He was relieved when she hopped onto the freeway and bypassed the most congested center city area. She drove south toward Daly City. Once on the freeway, Sonny dropped back even farther and selected a different lane, since it was easier to keep of track the Mercedes from a distance on the highway.

She pulled off the highway in Pacifica and drove directly to the parking lot at Mori Point on the shore. Sonny watched her park the Mercedes and lock it before walking toward the long tiered steps leading down the cliff toward the beach. She wore a pair of white capris, a red blouse, a yellow cardigan, Hermes scarf over her hair, and flat slip-on boat shoes.

Sonny snapped a picture of her walking away and thought about how he should proceed. Perhaps this was a rendezvous with her lover. It would be an opportunity to find them together, maybe catch a few quick snaps for evidence.

He scanned the parking lot. It was nearly empty, save for his car, Isabel's car, a beater fishing truck, and a VW Bug. If Isabel was meeting someone, he had a hard time imagining that person arriving in either vehicle. So, if he was there, how did he get there?

Sonny could see most of the steps, and a long stretch of the beach, but there were portions concealed from him by the cliff. He debated whether to follow Isabel on foot but doing that put him a great risk of blowing his secrecy. A man of Sonny's size and countenance was not easily forgotten. Once seen, he would be recognized in the future.

"This is just the first inning," he told himself. It was possible Isabel simply drove down to Pacifica to stroll on the beach. She was dressed casually enough. Maybe she was meeting a man, and maybe she wasn't. If she was, then she'd be back. It might take several days, or even a couple of weeks, but if this was her meeting point with a lover, she'd be back regularly, and that was a pattern. Patterns were good. They were predictable. It would have been a coup to uncover an illicit partner right out of the box, but it wouldn't have been terribly lucrative.

Sonny judiciously decided to stay in the car. He watched with binoculars as Isabel disappeared down the hill, until he could see only the bobbing scarfed top of her head, and then nothing at all.

If he couldn't risk spying on her on foot, the next best thing would be to record how long she remained at Mori Point. Having followed her all afternoon, her car was burned into his brain. After Isabel vanished from his view, Sonny drove the Kia from the parking lot and parked at a convenience store lot with a perfect view of the Mori Point lot exit.

She remained for almost an hour, before her car reappeared and turned left, back toward the freeway. Sonny waited for her to get a block or two ahead before he pulled in behind to follow her.

An hour wasn't much time, he thought. It didn't seem like a covert romantic assignation. When Isabel returned from her walk, her hair wasn't mussed under the scarf, and her clothes looked as perfectly pressed as before. Her makeup was undisturbed. Her trip to Pacifica simply didn't pass the illicit smell test.

It didn't matter. He was paid to follow her and report her whereabouts. She might return to Mori Point the next day or the day after. If she did, Sonny reminded himself to pack some tackle and some grungy clothes so he could pretend to be an ocean angler out for a relaxing afternoon of surf fishing. That way, he could observe her on those parts of the beach he couldn't see from the parking lot.

THIRTY-THREE

I trusted Sonny to do a creditable job of tailing the errant Ms. Standish without close supervision. I had nothing else on my plate, so after a sleepless night rolling the Brandon Hunt case around the inside my head, I decided to do something about it.

My first stop was the frat house where Mark Ballenger and Tony Richardson duked it out with a tulip poplar the night Hunt was attacked. The same stoner kid answered the bell, making me wonder whether he ever attended classes. Apparently, based on his clear eyes, I caught him before his morning wake and bake. I handed him my card.

"Dude," he said, after reading it. "Cops were already here."

"Come again?"

"You're here about Mark, right? Mark Ballenger?"

"That's right. I spoke with him about a month ago."

"That was you, man? Somehow I remembered you as bigger and meaner looking."

"It was me. Is Mark here?"

The kid gave me the stoner gawp. "You don't know. Geez. I thought you were here because…Well, look. Mark's missing. Nobody's seen him for, like, days."

"How many days?" I asked.

"Three. Maybe four. Nobody really thought much about it until the cops showed up."

"Which cops?"

"Just cops. Well, a detective, like you. Plain clothes, but with a badge and a gun."

"You recall what the detective looked like?"

"Sure. Heavy-set guy. Jowls like that cartoon dog. What's his name? Droopy."

Crymes. He must have been following up on the names I gave him.

"He came here looking for Mark?"

"Yeah. Just like you did. Wanted to talk to him about that fight at the kegger a few weeks back. Is that the damnedest thing? So much fuss over a little fight."

"And when the detective came to speak with him, that's when you realized Mark hadn't been around for days?"

"Yeah. I mean, we didn't think about it much. Sometimes people just take off. Go to the beach, or over to Tahoe. They don't always tell us when they go. It's not like we have sign out sheets around here. But when the detective came looking for him, nobody could remember seeing him for several days. He called for some backup, and they tossed Mark's room. Found his laptop computer, his suitcase, and all his clothes. A couple of the guys and I tried to call him, but his phone went straight to voicemail, like it was dead."

"Or turned off," I said.

"Now, why would anyone turn off their phone?"

I could see from his expression the concept distressed him.

"Phones contain GPS chips," I said. "If it's on, it's pinging off a cell tower nearby. You can find someone using their phone. Cops do it all the time."

"Radical," the kid said.

"Besides the detective who tossed Mark's room, have any other police been here to talk with Mark?"

"None that I know of."

As I suspected, Dexter Spears hadn't followed up on my tip. It figured.

"Keep my card," I said. "Call me if Ballenger shows up, okay?"

"Sure thing. Hey, is it really cool, being a private eye and all?"

"It's totally radical," I said.

In the car on the way back to my office, I called Detective Crymes. He answered on the first ring.

"What do you make of Ballenger's disappearance?" I asked.

"You know something about this?"

"I just heard."

"You aren't stomping around in my case, I hope."

I said, "Let's say my case and yours may intersect a little."

"You mean the stuff you were doing for Hunt that wasn't associated with the assault on campus?"

Busted.

"You've been talking to Dexter Spears."

"Boy's as dense as a green apple and lazy as a hillbilly bloodhound, but he remembers things. Can't figure why you're still doing whatever this is for Hunt. I don't think you're going to collect from his estate."

"I'm doing this for me. Unfinished business. Hunt fired me when the pictures were released. The thing I was doing was about the pictures."

"Extortion?"

"I don't know. It doesn't smell right. Whatever it was, though, I thought pretty strongly that Ballenger and Tony Richardson were involved."

"Thought? Or knew?"

"Just suspicions. That's why I handed them over to Spears. I figured, if he could pin them on the assault, they'd cop to whatever else was going on. We ran out of time, though. Whoever had the pictures released them before I could find out who they were. For all I know, Ballenger and Richardson were exactly who they claimed to be—a couple of jocks fighting over who really deserved to play shortstop."

"What made them look good for the Hunt assault?"

"The girl in the pictures? The blonde?"

"Yeah?"

"They were fighting over her at the frat house."

Silence for a few beats.

"Fuckin' coincidences," Crymes said. "You find out who she was?"

"Amy Beth Popowicz. Resident student, up from Pasadena."

"You said Popowicz?"

"Yeah."

"Hold on." I heard tapping on a computer keyboard. "Amy Beth Popowicz of Pasadena is the subject of a missing person report."

"Go figure," I said. "Let's do lunch."

THIRTY-FOUR

Pacifica is a five minute drive from my house in Montara. I had a feeling I'd learn more talking with Crymes than I would banging on doors, at least today. We met at a burger place in Pacifica and talked over a platter and a couple of Cokes.

"Who reported Amy missing?" I asked.

"Her roommate in the dorm. She contacted the campus cops when Amy didn't come home for three nights running. Same stonewall as the Ballenger kid. She tried calling Amy's phone, but it went right to voicemail."

"You want to bounce this around? Brainstorm explanations for two people going dark at the same time? I have all day."

"We both know there are only two answers. Either they've gone to ground, which looks incredibly suspicious."

"Or they've been taken off the game board," I said.

"Don't complicate my life."

"How long's she been missing?"

"four days. First I've heard of her. I'm getting all this off the BOLO put out by the campus cops. Seems I need to have a talk with their chief."

"His name's Ronald Couchell. Captain rank. Spears told me a month ago."

"How in hell do you remember this shit?" Crymes asked.

"Beats me. It's a gift. We need to find Tony Richardson," I said.

"You think? My leads are drying up here, Gold."

"I'm already in the university area banging on doors. Want me to try to run Richardson down? I need to talk to him anyway."

"Only if you call me the minute you catch up with him. I'm not real comfortable with the way your case is banging against mine as it is. Don't think you can run around like a badge-carrying swinging dick."

"Nothing uncomfortably graphic there," I said.

"You know what I mean. You've helped me in the past, and I know you're stand-up, so I'm cutting you a lot of slack here. Don't abuse it. And I want to know everything you find out that might be even remotely related to Hunt's death."

"Has the autopsy report come back yet?"

"Tox screen will take days, but the BAL was kind of elevated. Like DUI range. The CSI crew didn't lift any identifiable fingerprints except for Hunt's. No sign of a struggle. You familiar with the term *autoerotic asphyxiation?*"

"The Kung Fu Choke-Out?" I said. "Rough sex stuff. I've heard of it. You think Hunt accidentally cacked himself going for some kinky thrills?"

"We saw no evidence of anyone else in the house. We know he was drinking. If he mixed alcohol with some other substance, he might have passed out with the bag over his head and suffocated. Like I said, the medical examiner found no signs of struggle or obvious injuries. The man died from lack of oxygen. It's a hypothesis."

"I can see the bag part," I said. "But what's with the ball gag and the bindings? Not my scene, but my understanding is that's the sort of sex play that is better enjoyed with a partner."

"I didn't say it was a great hypothesis," Crymes said. "But facts are facts. The door wasn't forced. The windows were locked. There was no sign of violence. There was only one used drinking glass. Everything says Hunt was alone."

"But you aren't buying it."

"I'm not buying it. We know he was moved after death. Perhaps as much as an hour later."

"Okay. So we work backwards. Reverse engineer the scenario."

"I don't like making shit up, Gold. I prefer to go where the evidence leads."

"You've already jumped that ship, Detective."

He'd had his burger halfway to his mouth, but stopped, and lowered it back into the basket. He dredged a fry around in a pool of ketchup on the wax paper but didn't try to eat it. "Yeah. Guess I have at that."

"Here's what we know. However Hunt died, someone found him before the cops did. So we have Question One. Who was in the house with Hunt?"

"Which leads to *why*," Crymes said.

"Question Two. Question Three is…"

"When."

"So, let's toss out a couple of possible scenarios," I said. "Option One. Hunt is suddenly flush with television cash and decides to make it a party weekend. Booze, maybe some blow. We know he likes mollies, and they do not like alcohol. He hires an outcall hooker from the back of one of the tabloids, or maybe he swipes right on a kinky dating app, and Mistress Dry-Cleaning Bag shows up."

"Doesn't play," he argued. "No other DNA."

"She's wearing vinyl, and a wig."

"No prints."

"Gloves."

"Only one glass. He drank alone."

"Or she washed her glass and put it back in the cabinet after he died. Or she took it with her. Most highball glasses come in sets of four or eight. Find three or seven in his place, it's a possibility. So they drink a little, they pop some pills or snort some shit, and it's go time. Mistress trusses Hunt up, stuffs the ball gag into his mouth, and commences to do that voodoo that she do so well. But drug interactions work both ways. Maybe she puts the bag over Hunt's head, he passes out, and she slumps over, out cold. She wakes up some time later, and finds Hunt now soloing with the choir eternal. Maybe she rolls him over to check for a pulse, moving the body. She panics and boogies."

"You just sit around making this stuff up?" Crymes asked. "Because it's kind of spooky."

"A situation like that is tragic, and maybe she's on the hook for prostitution and leaving the scene of a crime, but otherwise…"

"It was an accident."

"And nothing to do with my thing over on the campus. Now, we have Scenario Two. The beatdown Hunt got at the college was part of an elaborate but woefully amateur extortion scheme run by students who reveled in the notion of passing him through a potato ricer. Amy Beth Popowicz is at the center of it. We know she slept with Hunt before, and the pictures on the Internet suggest she is swimming in the deep end of the kinky pool. I never found irrefutable proof she was involved, and I never told Hunt her name. So, a few weeks go by, and Hunt's been bounced from the college, so the kids got their way—"

"Wait," Crymes said. "That was their demand? That he quit?"

"Remind me never to let you get me in an interview room, Detective. Okay. Yeah. *Quit or we show these to the world.* They wanted him to resign, preferably in shame. Instead, they released the pictures, he got fired from the university, and became an immensely wealthy media darling."

"A Pyrrhic victory."

"Precisely. They won, but they felt like they lost. Now Hunt has an even larger megaphone to spout his garbage. So, Amy decides to take another bite out of the apple and get it right this time. She convinces Mark Ballenger to help her. Maybe Tony Richardson as well. For all I know, there's a

BOLO out on him as well. You didn't talk to him when you hit the frat house?"

"It was on my to-do list."

"So, she contacts Hunt and sucks up to him. *Oh, Brandon, I just can't forget our night together.* Stuff like that. Really gives his ego a handjob. She arranges to meet him someplace else. She gives him alcohol and drugs, and when he passes out she ties him up, gags him, and bags him. She and Mark and maybe Tony haul him back to his place in Pacifica and dump him. They put his prints on the glass, leave it next to him, and take off for parts unknown. If you've been following, Detective, that makes it murder."

"That's another hypothesis," Crymes said.

"Indeed it is," I said.

THIRTY-FIVE

It was too late to return to the city and get anything done at the university, so I headed south toward my Montara house instead. I called Heidi on the way. She thought steaks and wine on my deck overlooking the ocean sounded divine.

After dinner, I considered taking a few whacks at the new archtop project, but I couldn't get my head around it. Instead, I loaded the Art Tatum channel on Pandora, and relaxed on the couch, drinking wine and canoodling with Heidi. Apparently, I had a hard time keeping my mind on that as well.

"Enough," Heidi said eventually. "What's eating you?"

I settled back into the cushions. "Work stuff. Brandon Hunt's looking more like a murder all the time, and I have a feeling my case at the university might provide the break Crymes needs to close it."

"Let him do the legwork. He's still getting paid to."

"I'm not sure I gave Hunt full value for his money."

"So, you're seeking closure."

"Something like that. Stuff left undone weighs on me. What bothers me most is I liked Tony Richardson. Without going into too much detail, he might be a murderer. I thought I was a better judge of character."

"You did suspect him of beating up Hunt."

"There's a huge chasm between assault and murder. I didn't think Tony capable of jumping it. I'll try to run him to ground tomorrow. Hope he has an ironclad alibi for the night Hunt died. Something other than tussling with Mark Ballenger and punching a tree."

"What about Sonny?" she asked. "How's his divorce case going?"

"He's on the right track, I think. I don't know if she's cheating or not, yet, but she is up to some hinky shit. Stakeouts are exercises in patience. Sonny's good at patience. He plans to do a little disguise work at the beach in Pacifica tomorrow, give himself a closer look at why the wandering wife is visiting there. That is, if she goes there again. These cases are hard to predict."

"They involve people," she said. "We are an unpredictable animal."

"Her behavior today was suspicious enough. Never hurts to be prepared if she acts out of habit."

She cuddled up to me and laid her head on my chest. "I was ready for anything."

"Come again?"

"Banker, doctor, merchant marine..."

"Butcher, baker, candlestick maker?" I added.

"Used to get wet for soccer players and drummers," she said.

"Congratulations. Your girl card is in the mail."

"But a detective? Never crossed my mind. Nothing in my experience prepared me for you. Those other guys? In it for the bucks. You run on something different."

"I like getting paid. Gotta eat like everyone else," I said.

"Bullshit. You were on the job. Had a gold shield and everything. Dependable salary. A pension. All the crooks you could eat. By now you could be looking a cushy retirement down the barrel, but you tossed it away. It didn't give you what you needed."

"Funny. I was about to say that," I said.

"They couldn't hang with the code," she said.

That surprised me, mostly because it blew out the center of the X ring. Heidi startled me with the depth of her insight sometimes.

"The code," I said.

"So, what was missing on the force? Why'd you run like you stole it?"

"Your command of English idioms improves by the day," I said.

"Don't change the subject. It was the code, right?"

"Forget the code. You're obsessing on the code. I don't know what you're talking about."

"So, answer the question. Why'd you pull the ripcord on security?"

I refreshed our glasses. A nice Bordeaux. I stopped short of the dregs and opened its brother to finish the pour. I knew Heidi saw it for the stall it was. I needn't have bothered. She could wait me out. Eventually, she'd get her answer.

"I told you about my partner, Frank Raymond," I said.

She shuddered. I'd told her. What happened to Frank shouldn't happen to anyone, even if he did deserve it.

"There was a time Frank wasn't dirty," I continued. "He detested crooked cops. We both did. An inspector squad at SFPD is like anywhere else. You get all types—straight arrows, political favorites, action junkies, and a few lazy bums who reached their terminal career aspirations as soon as the city slapped a gold shield on their chest and became motivation-deprived. There are a thousand ways to slack off if you're in plain clothes. Inspectors—good ones—put in the hours needed. They knock on doors and wear out shoe leather and car warranties. Others take shortcuts."

"Bribes," she said.

"It always starts honestly. An inspector needs to talk to a suspect. Some bad guy, usually a guy with a lot of juice, can put the inspector and the suspect together, but he won't do it for free. So, the inspector gives the juicy guy something in return. Maybe it's fixing a traffic ticket. Maybe he goes soft on another less attractive suspect on less interesting charges. It's a little thing. It's always a little thing, but once that camel nose gets under the tent, they have you. Next time the cop comes asking for a favor, the bad guy does it for free, because they're buddies now, you see. Maybe a few weeks later, the bad guy shows up and says, *Hey. Remember that favor I did you?*"

"And it's payback time."

I shook my head. "Just setting the hook. The bad guy asks for a favor in return. The inspector protests, saying it's too much of a risk. The bad guy sweetens the pot with an

207

envelope of cash, or a baggie of blow, or a night with a top shelf hooker."

"Something small," Heidi said.

"At first. But now, Inspector Dumbass is compromised. And Bad Guy has proof."

"Inspector Dumbass has just crossed over to The Dark Side."

"I watched it happen a few times," I said. "After a while, I could see which guys were nibbling at the rat cheese. We all could. I even tried to help one guy not fall into the hole. He needed ready cash more than he wanted to see justice done, and in the end, it bit him too. I saw so many guys get sucked under, I wondered how long it would be before I made the list."

"Never," she said. "You're a straight arrow."

"So was Frank. See what I mean? Nobody gets a pass. Everybody is susceptible. Under the right circumstances, everyone is for sale. The worst part was when the corrupt guys started getting bumped up the promotion ladder. Now I was supervised by guys I knew were on the pad. One day, one of them ordered me to do something he shouldn't have. Instead, I gave him my badge and gun, and walked away. It was the right decision. He found someone else to do it and they were caught."

"Fired?"

"Demoted and transferred. The brotherhood never sacrifices its own. They give them bullshit assignments and wait for them to get the message, maybe, but no cop's career survives ratting on another cop or stomping another cop down the drain. I did good work on the job, made a small difference, but it was in the service of people to whom that didn't matter. I figured I would be more satisfied on my own."

"So you became a private cop."

"You dance with the one what brung you," I said. "By that point, my career options were limited. I had a very specific set of skills."

"Where have I heard that before?"

"You have a very specific set of skills yourself," I said.

"And, once again, your powers of deduction match your reputation," she said. "Want to interrogate me later?"

"I want to interrogate you right now," I said. "Whenever right now is."

She cuddled closer. "Ooh, Inspector!" she cooed.

THIRTY-SIX

Despite his South Pacific heritage, Sonny Malehala didn't care much for the ocean. He wasn't a beach bum by nature and thought sunbathing was a waste of time unless your ultimate goal was skin cancer. He also had little regard for fishing. His military training had taught him everything he needed to survive in and around water, and his father had taught him to fish, so he was perfectly competent, but that didn't mean he had to like it.

Mostly, Sonny didn't like the cold water splashing against his ankles as he stood on the beach at Mori Point with a surf rod and heavy test line, casting into the waves. To any passerby, he would appear to be a random surfcaster passing the day away. He wore baggy trousers with the cuffs rolled to mid-shin, a battered plaid flannel shirt, a shopworn fisherman's vest, and a floppy hat.

He had followed Isabel Standish again that morning. As soon as it became obvious she was again headed to Mori Point, Sonny pulled casually ahead of her on the freeway and into the distance. He arrived at the parking lot five minutes before she did, and quickly hauled his tackle down the shallow terraced steps to the strand to set up, so it would appear that he had been there for a while.

He sagged in a folding beach chair, the rod secured in a length of PVC pipe dug into the sand. He wore sunglasses, which allowed him to turn his head and watch the steps from the lot for Isabel to appear without looking as if he was watching. It didn't take long. She appeared at the top of the steps, wearing an untucked flowing yellow blouse over abstract print leggings. Instead of the scarf, she wore a cap. She also wore sunglasses, and for an instant Sonny wondered whether she was watching him as intently as he spied on her.

She made her way down the terraced hillside to the beach, and immediately turned left, away from Sonny.

"Well, shit," Sonny muttered. He'd guessed wrong. It was a coin toss as to which direction she would go. She'd picked heads. He'd called tails.

Sonny considered pulling up stakes and moving closer to the steps so he could keep an eye on her, but he didn't want to look suspicious. If necessary, he'd fish on the other side the next day. He trained a small set of binoculars from his vest pocket on her as she walked the beach, until she reached a shallow cove and disappeared behind a cliff. He folded the binoculars and put them away but continued watching. She had to come back sometime.

"Excuse me," someone said behind him. Sonny whirled around to face a tall, sturdy man wearing jeans, a sports shirt open at the collar, and a tweed jacket. The man's receding hair was dark brown shot through with gray, cut to just above the ears. He had the look of an ex-boxer, with a nose broken more than once and the faintest trace of cauliflower ear. He looked like he'd taken a few punches to the face over the years, but he smiled genially.

"Think you have something on your line," he said, pointing to the pole stuck in the PVC. The rod was bent nearly into a semicircle, the line as taut as a guitar string. Sonny grabbed it and started to reel it in.

"Mind if I watch?" the man asked.

"Suit yourself," Sonny said, as he fought the line. Whatever was on the other end preferred to stay where it was, and tugged back as strongly as Sonny pulled the rod. Even as he yanked the rod back and took up the reel slack, Sonny kept one eye on the south end of the beach, waiting for Isabel to reappear around the point. Just as he thought he had tired the fish on the end of the line, the rod went slack, the nylon line snapped under the tension.

"Aw, tough luck," the man said. "Might have been a shark, you know. They often bite through the line like that."

"Yeah," Sonny said absently, as he gathered his gear and kept an eye southward. "You might be right."

"You can relax. She won't be back for at least an hour," the man said.

Sonny turned to face him and waited. The man had hoped to surprise him, but Sonny was made of tougher stuff. One of two things was about to happen. The man would explain himself, and Sonny would learn something useful. In the other option, the man was protecting Isabel and intended to throw down right there on the beach. Sonny was ready for that as well.

The man held up a card. "Jack Delroy," he said. "I know your partner, Eamon Gold."

Sonny took the card. It read: *Sheldon Moon's Full Moon Security*. Under that, in a slightly smaller typeface, it read *Jack Delroy, Operative*.

"You're a PI?" Sonny asked.

"Why? I don't look like one?"

"You're working for—" Sonny nodded toward the south.

"Isabel Standish. Normally, I wouldn't divulge that, but she insisted. I told her it was a bad idea."

"It is."

"Glad you think so. Clients, though. Right?"

"Tell me about it. They're the worst. So, when did you make me?"

"In the parking lot outside Isabel's neighborhood. But I saw Gold at the Pampas Club, so I knew he was working for Standish. Didn't know he'd taken on a partner."

"Sonny Malehala," he said. "Got a card up in the car. Mine has a big eye on it."

"Classy," Delroy said. "So you're employed by Alan Standish."

"Let's go with that for now. You're here keeping an eye on the missus, instead of bird-dogging the old man, so you aren't doing divorce surveillance. I'm familiar with Sheldon Moon as well. Your agency specializes in protection for the G5 private jet set. Who are you protecting her from?"

"Isabel? Nobody. Her boyfriend, though..."

"So she is stepping out on Standish?"

"Wouldn't you?"

"Never met the man. Eamon did the initial interview."

"He's a bit of a stuffed shirt," Delroy said. "We need to talk, and I need a beer. Isabel's on a long walk. There's a diner up the road a bit. Let's go grab a bite and a brew and talk about our mutual interests. I promise she won't leave before we get back."

It might have been the big break in the case, and an opportunity for Sonny to prove to Gold that he was ready to work on his own. It might have been a trap. Mostly, Sonny decided, it was a chance to escape the damned Pacific Ocean water freezing his feet.

"Sure." He gathered his tackle.

———————

Delroy ordered a plate of loaded nachos and a Coors. Sonny settled for iced tea. Delroy examined Sonny's business card.

"It really has an eye on it."

"Don't look at me," Sonny said. "I didn't design it."

"You not eating?"

"My mother told me never to order lobster on the first date," Sonny said.

Delroy scooped nachos onto a side plate with his fork and gestured for Sonny to have some. Sonny didn't want to appear unfriendly, so he loaded his plate as well. He was gratified when he took a bite to discover they were pretty darned good.

"You mentioned Isabel's boyfriend," Sonny said.

"Now, there's a man with a lot on his mind," Delroy said, and he pounded back half the schooner of beer in one gulp. He signaled to the waitress for a refill. "Your client wouldn't mind seeing him on the first plane to Argentina carrying a bomb in the hold."

"You mean Gavrillo Weber."

"Standish told you Weber embezzled a substantial amount of money from his law firm's accounts."

"And?"

"You're not bad at this, you know? I mean, for a rookie. Did Gold ever tell you how he and I met?"

"No."

"I made him on a stakeout. Just like you."

"Congratulations. You must be very good."

"I get by. And I know when someone's sucking up to me. Relax. Everyone gets made sooner or later. Goes with the territory."

"Eamon said the same thing."

"Well, he's been at this for a long time. He knows the ropes. What do you want to know about Weber?"

"Why?"

"Why what?"

"Why do you want to share information? We're on opposite sides of this thing."

"Sonny," Delroy said. "We aren't even playing the same game. You and Eamon were hired by a real piece of work. Alan Standish has you snookered. Go ahead. Ask me anything."

"Did Weber steal money from the law firm?"

"No. Next question."

"Did *anyone* steal money from the law firm?"

"Excellent question. Yes. Someone stole money from the law firm." He drained the beer just as the waitress arrived with a refill.

"You plan on driving home?" Sonny asked.

"Got this weird metabolism. I can torpedo three cans of beer and never blow close to point-zero-four. Seriously. I've done breath tests on myself. Weird as shit."

"How does Isabel figure in?"

"Very good. Misdirection and redirection. Police training?"

"Military. Ranger."

"Finest kind. Your client's suspicions are well-founded. Isabel Standish is humping Gavrillo Weber and has been for some time. Only problem is, those suspicions were confirmed long before you and Eamon entered the story. Why did Standish tell you he hired Weber?"

"He was brought up from Argentina to ride ponies for the Pampas Polo Club. To get the work visa, Standish gave him a position at the firm," Sonny said.

"Nice cover story. Gavrillo Weber was hired mostly to service Isabel Standish. He's an excellent polo rider as well, which plays nicely into the cover story. The job at the firm, though. That was a masterpiece. Standish knows all about Isabel and Weber. He's known about them for quite a while. He likes to watch."

Sonny did the eyebrow thing.

"You got quite a tell there, Sonny," Delroy said.

"Why I never gamble. I suppose he already has pictures and videos to validate the affair."

"Peepers are always like that. Take a picture. It'll last longer. Problem is, after a while, Isabel discovered she had more in common with Weber than with Alan. Alan's not stupid. And Isabel is loaded. She's the real money in the family. That's why Alan brought Weber to California in the first place. They met at a polo tournament in the lower hemisphere. Alan's flopper was already on the disabled list, but he liked to keep Isabel and her enormous bank account happy, so they made an arrangement. She first slept with Weber in Buenos Aires, while Alan relaxed in the hotel lounge with an Old Fashioned. Weber must be quite the cocksman because the woman became his number one fan. She convinced Alan to bring him to San Francisco, put him out to stud."

"Well," Sonny said, as the waitress refilled his tea. "Nothing sordid there."

"Lifestyles of the rich and famous," Delroy said, with a shrug. "Whatcha gonna do? Who knew the two crazy kids were gonna fall in love? Anyway, Isabel's money enables Full Moon to hide Weber somewhere you'll never find him."

"Challenge accepted," Sonny said.

"Don't waste your time. Besides, you have bigger things to worry about. Isabel is really pissed at her husband. She noticed he was buying a lot of polo equipment and new ponies of late and asked for money from her to pay for them. She discovered he was asking for far more than the equipment and ponies cost. This was where Standish really was clever. By framing Weber for embezzlement and having him deported, he would break the bond between Weber and Isabel, and hold on to his access to her money."

"I assume you have proof of all this," Sonny said. "We're not playing he said / she said here, are we?"

"Weber isn't your garden variety patsy," Delroy said. "Seems the kid has mad accounting skills he learned while in school in Argentina. He made copies of the records that could put Standish in jail for a long time—including the attempt to frame him—and went underground with them."

"They're his insurance policy," Sonny said.

"Your client is a very bad man. He hired you to find out if his wife was cheating on him, when he already knew she had a lover. He tried to frame the lover, to get him out of Isabel's life—not because she was in love with another man, but because Standish would lose his private treasure trove and all the goodies. You asked earlier what I'm protecting Isabel from? You. My job is to intercept anybody her husband tosses her way and keep them from following her to Weber."

"You can't keep playing this game forever," Sonny said. "Sooner or later, Weber has to surface."

"Sooner," Delroy said. "At Sheldon's suggestion, Weber's going to the state Bureau of Investigation. It'll go to the grand jury soon. It's safer for Weber to stay in hiding, for now, until Standish is taken into custody."

"I take it Isabel has no intention of meeting with Weber until then?"

"She's taking one for the team. I hear she's clawing at her wallpaper at night. I've been hanging out at the Pampas Club whenever she's there. That's how I saw Gold meeting with Standish the other day. From that point on, my job was to follow her to see if anyone else was following her. And here you are. You want some advice?"

"Okay."

"Tell Standish you found proof Isabel is having an affair. Write your report. Deliver it. He isn't going to divorce her. Wouldn't dare. Cash the check quickly because his accounts may be frozen any day."

THIRTY-SEVEN

"Well, shit," I said, after Sonny relayed his conversation with Jack Delroy. "We're the bad guys."

"We're patsies," Sonny said. He slouched in the chair on the other side of my desk. "We were played by both sides."

"It happens," I said. "So, what do you plan to do now?"

"Me?"

"It's your case, partner. Your nest is a distant memory. Fly away, little starling. Fly fly fly."

"Did Delroy really make you?"

"Yeah, but I made him back. I was running down a kid in Daly City, a serial blackmailer. Full Moon was working for another one of the victims. We both staked out the kid's house. Delroy saw me first. I made him about five minutes later. Heidi and I pulled a trick on him, which was how I found out he worked for Sheldon Moon. You're stalling."

Sonny waved at the air. "Guess I could use some advice."

"What are your options?"

"One: Write the report, take the cash, and run."

"Why won't it work?" I said.

"Standish doesn't give a damn whether Isabel is cheating. He isn't interested in divorce evidence."

"So, when you tell him his wife is thumping about with Gavrillo Weber?"

"He'll want Weber."

"Preferably his head on a pike, from what you've told me. At that point, you have two options. What are they?"

"Take the case or refuse it."

"Why refuse it? Seems like a nice payday, especially if Weber is dug in somewhere. Lots of billable hours."

"Which we may never collect if Standish is arrested and his accounts frozen," Sonny said.

"So how do you explain quitting the case?"

Sonny rubbed his palms together. Somewhere nearby, a seismograph needle jumped. "I guess this is where I need the advice."

"I'm not going to tell you anything you don't already know," I said. "You spent several years working for very bad people."

"Yeah?" I could hear the defensiveness in his voice. Sonny had always been sensitive about working for mobsters.

"Were you completely in the dark regarding what they did for a living?"

"Never. Not for a second."

"But you kept working for them."

"We've been over this, Eamon. The money was good, and I was never involved in the illegal end of their business."

"Until you showed up in my office with your pistol pointed at my face. Nobody rides for free with the mob, Sonny. Sooner or later, you're either all in or cashed out. I don't have to tell you that. That's not my point, anyway.

You kept working because they were your employer. I asked you the first time we met whether you could just quit. You thought you could. Maybe you were right. My point is this. Standish is your client. You aren't married to him. You do owe him confidentiality, though. When you take his money, you agree to tell him the truth. You have evidence confirming his wife is sleeping with another man. That's what he hired you to find out. In the course of your investigation, you've learned he's facing indictment. Tell him that as well. We don't lie to our clients. Tell him everything you know, and everything you think. If he asks you to go after Weber, you either do it or quit. If he asks why you quit, tell him the truth, that you have reason to believe he's using you to get to Weber so he can cover up his own crimes."

"And what then?"

"That's up to Standish. You need to cover your ass, though. Document everything in your notes. Every conversation, every phone call, every surveillance. From what Delroy said, the feds are involved now. They're very good at what they do. They'll find out Standish hired us, and they're going to want to know what you knew and when you knew it. I'm sure Mr. Bugliosi warned you about fooling around with the feds. What happens between you and Standish stays between you, until you get a subpoena or court order. Our clients' rights to privacy end there, and the feds love tossing around subpoenas."

"One problem," Sonny said.

"Yeah?"

"I don't have direct evidence of Isabel's infidelity. Only proof I have of an affair between Isabel and Weber is Jack Delroy's word. I never saw them together. What I do next depends on whether Delroy is stand-up. Can I trust what he says?"

"He's old school. The real deal. I saw him take five slugs in the vest a couple of years back, and he was up and jogging minutes later. I don't care much for his boss, Sheldon Moon, but Delroy's okay. So, you got this? I have some stuff to do over at the university today."

"I got it. I'll meet with Standish later today. You still working the Hunt thing? Thought your buddy Crymes was handling it."

"Hunt never made a complaint about the extortion, and even told me he didn't want the police to know. Crymes figured it out, so I gave him just enough not to violate Hunt's privacy. He has me on a tight leash, though."

"Can't figure out why you're putting in expensive hours for a guy who's never going to pay."

"He already paid," I said. "I didn't finish the job."

———

Sonny had seen Ballenger and Richardson at an apartment belonging to Plyler and Dean. Apartment 1G, Building Thirty-Six Hundred Two. Took me about five minutes to locate the front door, which I rapped on sharply.

The door opened about half a foot. A pale face peered out at me. I held up my card.

"You must be Mr. Plyler," I said.

He took the card and squinted at it.

"Dean," he said. "Phil isn't here."

"Even better," I said. "Invite me in."

"What?"

"Ask me to step inside, so I don't stand out on your front stoop looking like a schmuck."

"What do you want?"

"I need to talk to you about your roommate and a couple other guys," I said. "Won't take ten minutes."

"What other guys?" he said.

"What's your first name?" I asked.

"Alex."

"Okay, Alex. You're Alex Dean, and your roommate is Philip Plyler. Right?"

"Yeah..."

I held up a print of the picture Sonny had taken. "This is you and your roommate meeting with two other students named Mark Ballenger and Tony Richardson. It was taken about a month ago. Ballenger and Richardson are suspects in the assault of Professor Brandon Hunt a few weeks back. The police already have their full names, and they know about you and Phil. Talking to me might help you avoid a visit from a real cop."

It wouldn't, if I was right, but he didn't need to know that.

He thought it over, and in the end, he made the right decision—that is, the one that made my job easier. He opened the door and allowed me to enter.

It was a typical off-campus student apartment. Thrift store furniture, an oversized flat screen, metal rock posters on the walls. The place had a burned-in aroma of stale weed smoke, body spray, fermentation, and infrequent laundering. Shit hadn't changed a bit in the quarter century since I was in college. Alex Dean plopped down on a stained sofa. I elected to stand. Seemed safer that way. He was long and lean, like a track sprinter. His hair was cut close to the scalp. His eyes were so dark it was hard to see the borders of his pupils. He had about a pound of metal imbedded in his nose, lip, eyebrow, ears, and lord knows where else. He looked like the poster boy for parental disapproval.

"Tell me what you know about Amy Beth Popowicz," I said.

"Thought you wanted to talk about Mark and Tony."

"It's a package deal. On the same night these pictures were taken, you were all seen in the company of Ms. Popowicz."

"Yeah. I know her," he said. His voice was surly.

"How'd you meet?"

"Tony. He knew her first."

Curious. Ballenger and Richardson had suggested that Tony met Amy at the kegger.

"How long?"

"Beats me." He shrugged. "I never asked. But Tony introduced her to us all."

"How do you know Ballenger?"

"Tony. He introduced us."

"Did you witness a fight between Mark Ballenger and Tony Richardson at Ballenger's frat house?" I asked.

"Naw, man, but I heard about it."

"Were you at the party the night the fight happened?"

"No. I was somewhere else."

"Where?"

"Damned if I can recall. I just know I wasn't at that party."

I held out the picture again. "They seem to have made up."

"Yeah," Dean said, smirking. "How 'bout that?"

"Are you a student at the university?" I asked.

"Thought you wanted to know about Mark and Tony. You're sure asking a lot of questions about me."

"It all goes in the same pile."

He tried to stare me down. Many have tried. Few have succeeded. He wasn't one of them. I stared back and waited. Miles Davis once commented on the importance of playing the silences. I was pretty good at is well. He cracked before the first minute ended. "All right. I dropped out, okay? Didn't register at the end of the last semester. My parents don't know."

"Sounds like you have some big problems. I take it your parents sent you money for tuition and books. Not a lot to live on for an entire semester. You working?"

"Looking, man. People see my face and slam their doors."

"Maybe lose some of the hardware."

"You have to be so judgy?"

"I'm not, but your potential employers probably will be. Read the room, kid. When did you see Mark Ballenger last?"

"Last week sometime. Tuesday, maybe."

"And Amy Popowicz?"

"Same time. They were together."

"Okay, Alex. I'm going to toss one of the big ones at you. It's really important that you tell me the truth, because Mark and Amy and Tony might be gummed up in a murder case. Also, if you lie to me, I'll find out, and I guarantee you the cops will come down on you like a bag of dumbbells. You understand?"

"Sure. I'm not stupid."

"We'll leave that discussion for another time. Were you among the people who beat up Professor Brandon Hunt on the night Mark and Tony fought at the frat house?"

Dean grinned. "That's what this is about? Shit, man. You're tossing around words like murder and had me worried. No, man. I wasn't there. Okay?"

"All right," I said.

"But I know someone who was," he added.

THIRTY-EIGHT

"You mean, besides Mark and Tony?"

He grinned. "Did I say they were there?"

"I'm saying they were there. Are you telling me I'm wrong? Are you trying to be cute?"

I gave him the mean look, the one that scares birds out of the trees. He was rattled.

"Okay. They were there. Tony asked me to join them, but I begged off. Sounded like a clusterfuck to me."

"What about your roommate? Phil? Was he in on it?"

Alex gnawed at a thumbnail for a few seconds. "Yeah. Phil was in on it."

"Where is Phil, right this moment?"

More chewing. I thought I saw a glint of tears at the corner of his eye. "I don't know, man. He's been gone several days. Tell you the truth, I'm getting a little worried."

"Was Phil here when Mark and Amy visited last week?"

"They came to see him. I was just hanging here."

He stared at me for a bit, as if he thought I was done. He was wrong.

"Are you going to make me drag this out of you?" I asked. "Because I have all day, and I know you don't have a job or classes to run off to. How long after Mark and Amy visited did Phil take off?"

"Like, maybe an hour or two."

"Did he say where he was going?"

"Just to meet them. And Tony."

"Tony Richardson," I clarified.

"Yeah. Mark said they had to do something important, and Tony was waiting for them. He didn't say where, though."

I had a feeling I knew where. The biggest hitch in the Brandon Hunt murder, according to Detective Crymes, was the issue of whether Hunt had died in his beach shack. What I had learned made that less likely. Four people can move a body with relative ease, and we already knew Hunt was moved after death. It sounded like Tony had summoned his posse to the place where Hunt really died.

"Have you found Tony Richardson yet?" I asked Crymes over the phone after I left Alex Dean's place.

"Haven't checked on him. Snagged another case late last night. We're short-handed, so I'm juggling them."

"I just finished interviewing a kid named Alex Dean. His roommate is named Phil Plyler."

"Yeah. I recall those names from the report Inspector Spears filed. They're on my call list as well."

"Plyler's missing," I said. "For four or five days now. He took off the same night as Mark Ballenger and Amy Beth Popowicz. I'm going to run down Tony next, but I bet I come up empty with him as well. There's more. This Dean kid told me Plyler, Ballenger, and Richardson were all in on the assault on Hunt, along with players to be named later."

"And you think Amy Popowicz was involved as well."

"If I'm right, she's the ringleader. There's someone else I need to talk to today. Her name's Sandy Dennis."

"The actress?"

"No. A student. The other girl in the Brandon Hunt photos. She picked Amy Popowicz' profile out on Tinder. That's just too random to be coincidence."

"Unless that's what triggered the entire thing," Crymes said. "You interviewed Popowicz, right?"

"Yeah. She claimed she didn't know who Hunt was. When Sonny and I told her, she seemed genuinely disgusted to find out she'd shagged the modern equivalent of Josef Goebbels."

"Did you know her major is theater?"

"Do tell."

"You don't sound surprised," Crymes said.

"I ran out of surprise on this case days ago. If she's any good, she could have fooled us." A thought occurred to me. "Wait. You know her major?"

"Part of the missing person investigation the campus police are conducting. They keep records of this stuff."

"Both Sandy Dennis and Tony Richardson are psych majors. Makes me wonder about Phil Plyler and Mark Ballenger. Maybe I'll check into it. Did you talk with Chief Couchell about the missing person report again yet?"

"No."

"Mind if I meet with him? I was supposed to a few weeks back—something Dexter Spears set up—but Hunt fired me before I could talk to him. Same deal. I ask him about my thing, and I'll share whatever I get from him that spills over onto your turf."

"Don't make me regret this, Gold."

"One other thing. We now have four people who went missing before Brandon Hunt died. One dead guy would be a light load for that many people. It explains how he was moved after he died."

"He was killed somewhere else," Crymes said.

"And I think Tony Richardson knows where. All I have to do is find him."

THIRTY-NINE

The seats in Alan Standish's office waiting room were not made for comfort—at least, not the comfort of a person the size of a professional wrestler. Sonny tried to find a position that didn't either squeeze him or twist him out of shape. The secretary watched him from the corner of her eye, with a hint of amusement on her face.

Her phone buzzed. She answered it and placed the receiver back in the cradle. "Mr. Standish will see you now," she said, and gestured toward Standish's door.

Standish's office was an exercise in self-adulation. California claro walnut wainscoting covered the bottom half of every wall. Above that, the walls were festooned with framed certificates and pictures. Three degrees were framed behind Standish's desk. On another wall were hung pictures of Standish cozying up to some major movers and shakers. A couple of governors. An Oscar winning actor or two. Every mayor of San Francisco dating back thirty years. Sonny's former mob boss JuneBug, which was kind of a surprise. A glass-front case against one wall housed dozens of polo trophies.

Standish stood behind his desk.

"We haven't met," he said. "Only on the phone."

"Sonny Malehala." He handed Standish his card. "You've met my partner, Mr. Gold, though."

"Yes. At my club in Tiburon. He was there with the most delightful woman. Helga?"

"Heidi."

"Of course. My mistake. I was surprised when he decided to hand the case over to you."

"He's working on another matter that demands a great deal of time. I could give you my complete attention," Sonny said.

Standish clasped his hands together on his desk blotter. "So. Have you discovered anything important?"

"Several things. First, your wife has hired another private investigation agency."

Standish leaned back in his chair. "She has?"

"Full Moon. I had lunch with their operative yesterday. I was maintaining surveillance on your wife. He was doing the same on me. He confirmed that your wife is having an affair, Mr. Standish. But I don't think that comes as much of a surprise for you."

"Beg pardon?"

"You've known about Isabel and Gavrillo Weber for some time. You brought him up from Argentina to ride a hell of a lot more than a polo pony. My partner, Mr. Gold, has a rule when it comes to clients. They get three lies. After that, we walk. You've used two of yours already."

"When have I lied?"

"When you hired us to tail your wife for having an affair you not only know about, but condone, and sometimes participate in as a voyeur."

That rattled him. Color rose in his face. Sonny knew he had hit the right nerve.

"You...you investigated *me?*" Standish shouted.

"No. But Full Moon has. I'm just the beneficiary of their legwork. Lie Number Two: Gavrillo Weber never embezzled a penny from your firm. You want him for another reason. You need Weber to disappear, and the sooner the better."

"And why would I want that?"

"Because he can put you away for a long, long time and destroy your career. I am obligated under our agency agreement to inform you that the California Bureau of Investigation is amassing an impressive file on you. Indictments appear to be on the horizon."

"For what?"

"Embezzlement, for starters. Weber has immunity, and he walked out of here with enough documentation to make you a prison lawyer. In my opinion, if your goal in finding Weber was to force him back to Argentina, you have nothing left to threaten him. Under his immunity agreement, he gets a pass even if he really was skimming the client accounts. But we both know he wasn't, don't we?"

Standish turned and stared out the window.

"There's more," Sonny said.

"What could be worse?" Standish said.

"Isabel knows you've been stealing from her. She knows you lied and inflated the costs of your polo hobby, and you've been using the excess money to cover your own skimming of client accounts."

"That bitch," Standish growled. "She's going to get away with it."

"I suppose, since you're still my client, I should say *get away with what?*"

"You haven't met my lovely wife?"

"I've observed her only from a distance," Sonny said.

"Beautiful, right?"

"I've seen worse. Is this going somewhere?"

Standish stood and walked to the window overlooking midtown San Francisco. "It might be easier to simply jump out the window," he said.

"Quicker, certainly," Sonny said.

"My wife is beautiful," he repeated. "And she is cunning and devious and mean. There are parts missing in her head you can't get spares for. I'm a kept man, Malehala. Sure, my practice is successful, but the entire firm's yearly gross looks puny next to the annual dividends from her family holdings. She needed social connections, though, and I am a social animal. The arrangement worked perfectly for years."

"Until your dangle lost its angle."

Standish turned back to him. "God, you're a vulgar man."

"Tall words from a man who bought a boytoy for his wife and then watched himself get cuckolded."

"You've got it all wrong. Yeah. I've had some issues in the marital department. I have a medical problem that makes the blue pill risky. Isabel is a…well, she's a vibrant, vital woman. She has needs. I mean, like, *needs*. She runs hot and cold, but when things heat up, she's insatiable. I, on the other hand, am unavailable to satisfy her."

"See a sex therapist."

"She wouldn't hear of it. I tried…things. Techniques. Toys. Alternate methods of stimulation."

"Too much information," Sonny said.

"Let's say, then, that I made every attempt to cater to her desires, but nothing worked."

"She only wanted the Big Bowanga."

"In the final analysis, yes. Our marriage suffered as a consequence. She had affairs with a few of our acquaintances during her hypomanic frenzies. It became awkward in the dressing room at the club. Then, in Buenos Aires, she met Gavrillo. It was lust at first sight. I think she shagged him the first night they were introduced."

"As legend has it, you rode that one out in the bar downstairs."

"True enough. I'm not proud of it. They didn't deceive me. I knew exactly what was going on upstairs. I chose to ignore it. I told you, Mr. Malehala, she has a dark streak, especially when she's in heat. She insisted I invite Gavrillo to join us at dinner the next evening, where we depleted the wine cellar's malbec supply. We were all juiced. Next thing I knew, we were in our suite. I collapsed on the sofa, semi-comatose, staring while she and Weber went at it on the rug in front of the fireplace. Tantalizing me seemed to thrill her. She insisted on doing it again. And again."

"What did that suggest to you?"

"She was trying to drive me away. She had her connections, and a man who could satisfy her, so I had become supernumerary. I became convinced of it when we flew back to San Francisco, and three days later she demanded I recruit Gavrillo for the polo squad and bring him north. She even demanded I give him a job with the firm, to legitimize his presence in the country. It was obvious there was more than just animal magnetism between them. I could see it. My wife was falling in love."

"But you love the money and the stuff, so you gave in."

"I was in…financial difficulty."

"This is why you skimmed your client accounts."

"Borrowed, more precisely."

"Until you could defraud enough money from your wife to cover the missing cash," Sonny said.

"*Defraud* is a harsh word. With the humiliation she'd put me through, I was due a little gravy. She owed me. So, yeah, I inflated the polo costs. I repaid all the accounts and altered the records to conceal what I had done."

"And then, having become an expert at embezzlement, you realized you had found a way to get rid of your wife's paramour," Sonny said. "You doctored the records to make it look as if Weber was skimming instead of you."

"What would you do, Mr. Malehala?"

"Not *that,*" Sonny said.

"I suspect we are made of different stuff," Standish said. "Somehow, Isabel found out what I was doing. Probably from Weber. She came to my office. Sat right where you are now. She said she'd ruin me. No, that's not right. She said

237

she'd *destroy* me. The next day, Weber disappeared. Isabel still lived in our house, but she took to sleeping in a spare bedroom on the second floor. We haven't spoken in days. I didn't tell Mr. Gold everything at our first meeting. How could I, without placing my own head in the noose?"

"I know Eamon," Sonny said. "He would have refused the job."

"Which leads to the same conclusion. Either way, Isabel wins. She destroyed me to keep Gavrillo."

"Dude," Sonny said. "You destroyed yourself. I think you're a relatively inoffensive guy who was unfortunately born without a spine. You got in a jam and made compromises that jacked you up against the karma wall. When faced with the choice of keeping your dignity or a wad of cash, you doubled down like a blackjack junkie. And then you committed a felony to keep the party rolling, and then another. I don't know what to say, man, except I would hate to be inside your skin right now. So, I'll just ask. Is there anything more our agency can do for you?"

"You seem to have done quite enough."

Sonny took an envelope from his inside jacket pocket and slid it across Standish's desk.

"What is it?" Standish asked.

"The invoice for our services, including a breakdown of expenses with copies of the receipts and a complete written report of our findings to date. Minus, of course, what you told me in this conversation. If you like, I can send the amended report to you later today. No extra charge."

"Ah," Standish said, as he looked over the pages. "That…won't be necessary."

"I have to document the conversation anyway," Sonny said. "If you want a revised report, contact our office. Under the circumstances, I'd appreciate a check today if you don't mind."

FORTY

I called the campus police office at the university first thing the next morning. Chief Couchell was out of pocket for the day, attending a conference in Sacramento. I made an appointment to meet with him the next day and decided to cruise over to the campus to look for Tony Richardson.

I had just climbed behind the wheel and started the car when my phone rang. The Bluetooth screen on my dash said it was Sonny.

"You meet with Standish?" I asked.

"Got the check in my jacket pocket," he said.

"He decided to cut us loose?"

"There's not much we can do for him anymore. Before he's finished, the only person who can help him will be a priest. He confirmed everything Delroy told me, and then some. He put an interesting personal spin on the story."

"Made himself out to be the victim?"

"How'd you guess?"

"He's the type. So, how'd you like your first case?"

There was a long silence on the line.

"Sonny? You still there?"

"Sorry. I was thinking. It wasn't what I expected."

"What do you mean?"

"I thought there would be more of a sense of...closure."

"What did you expect?" I asked. "Guns blazing and feds breaking down the door?"

"There was no climax," Sonny said. "He wrote me a check, and it was over. There were no heroes. It was just squalid and sordid."

"Squalid and sordid keeps groceries on our table, Bub," I said. "Eighty percent of the cases we take will be zero sum games. Usually, nobody wins in the end. It sucks, but them's the breaks. What you need to learn is to detach yourself from that. You're an observer in the process. You're the Greek chorus ripping the hide off tragic characters. You're immune from their squishy fates. At the end of the day, you get to check out of their hell and go home. They're strapped in for the whole ride."

"Tolstoy," Sonny said. *"Every happy family is the same. Every unhappy family is unhappy in their own way."*

"And *viva la différence*," I said. "It's that tragic diversity that keeps the conversation lively in our business. People don't get into the peeper game for the regular hours and the routine."

"So, you need any help with your case?" he asked.

"No. Take the day. Write up the Standish report tomorrow. You did a good job on this one, Sonny. Soon as you pile up enough hours, I think you're ready to get your full license and go indie if that's what you want. I won't say it hasn't been helpful to have you working under my shingle, though."

"Let's take it case by case," he said. "I'm in no rush. Hey, maybe I'll go to work for Sheldon Moon."

"Then I *will* shoot you," I said.

I was lucky to find Earleen Marley in her office. She smiled as I walked through the door.

"Eamon," she said, as she stood and hugged me. "An unexpected pleasure."

"Nice to see you, too," I said.

"And a coincidence. I just got off the phone with Sonny. We're meeting for dinner tonight and whatever."

"The whatever should be fun. He's likely pumped up. He just wrapped his first solo case."

"He told me. Not about the case, of course. But he said it was closed. Successfully, I presume?"

"The fee is a thing of beauty."

She laughed. I liked Earleen's laugh.

"So, to what do I owe the pleasure?" she asked.

"I need you to bend the rules a little."

"You know I'm always game for a little subversion. What's up?"

"I'm still working the Brandon Hunt case."

That surprised her. "Brandon's dead."

"Like Jacob Marley, there is no doubt whatever about that."

"I thought you were just providing protection for him after the assault," she said.

"It evolved from there. I'm trying to locate a student I interviewed a month ago. I know you professors have access to student information. I was hoping you could look up his address for me."

"I don't know, Eamon..." she said.

"It's just a tiny subversion."

She pursed her lips and stared me down, but quickly relented. "Just the address."

"I'll do the legwork from there."

"What's the name?"

"Tony Richardson."

She had already turned to her keyboard, but she froze when I said Tony's name.

"I know him," she said. "He's a psych major. Works in my research partner's lab. How's Tony involved?"

"I'm afraid I can't say. It's possible he's gone missing."

"Missing? How?"

"That's part of what I can't talk about. A couple of students related to the work I did for Hunt are off the grid. I don't know whether they're missing voluntarily. Tony was in their same situation, I think. I need to find him, first of all, to make sure he's safe."

"Of course," she said. "You would. It's what you do. I found his address."

She wrote it down for me on a sticky note. I attached it to my wallet and put it in my pocket.

"Still feeling rebellious?" I asked.

"What are you suggesting?"

"I need the majors of a couple of other students."

"Just their majors?"

"That's all."

"Hell, ask them in a bar. That's the number one pickup line on this campus."

"Any campus," I said. "How about Mark Ballenger?"

Her fingers stopped on the keyboard. "Marky Mark."

"Say again?"

"His nickname in the department. We'd never say it to his face. He's a psych major, Eamon. He's one of Doctor Soderquist's advisees, and he's working in Doctor Skibbe's cognitive lab."

"Phil Plyler?"

She leaned forward. "Eamon, you're scaring me. I know all these kids. What's this about?"

"I don't know, yet. It's all still murky. But I can tell you Ballenger and Plyler are in the wind. Nobody has seen them in over a week. And I can tell you that Tony is a suspect in the assault on Hunt before he was murdered. I need to talk to him, as soon as possible."

"I can't believe this," she said. "What you're describing— it sounds like a conspiracy."

"If they're all missing of their own accord. The alternative is a lot worse," I said.

FORTY-ONE

Tony Richardson lived off campus in a time-worn strip of studio apartments built around a central parking lot. I'd interviewed a person there before. They were tiny but cheap, consisting of a single room and an attached bathroom the size of a linen closet. The exterior was the most boring brick ever fired, and the interior walls were painted cinderblock. They were roach motels for people. Most of the tenants were students.

Tony's front door was cheap painted plywood with three filthy windows set on a diagonal and no peephole. I rapped on the door and waited. Nobody answered. I tried again, with the same result. I wrote a note on the back of one of my business cards and slipped it into the jamb.

There were lots of explanations for his absence. He might be in class. Being an athlete in training, he might be at the gym working out. He might be grabbing a bite at the student center food court. He might be rotting in the trunk of a junked Monte Carlo in a scrapyard. The possibilities were endless.

The baseball coach at the university, Marvin Lee, sat behind his office desk in the gym when I knocked on his door. He looked like most coaches—former jocks gone halfway to suet but still clinging to the hope for more glory. He was six feet even, with close-cropped blonde hair that I suspected had benefitted from drugstore coloring. His eyes were a deep blue, sunken deep in their sockets. He wore the standard issue sports shirt with the university logo, gym pants, and sneakers. As I rapped on the door jamb, he seemed lost in papers strewn on his desk. For all I could tell, he might be doing his taxes. He looked up.

"Help you?" He had a voice straight out of a beef commercial.

I passed him my card.

"Private detective?"

"I'm checking up on a couple of your players," I said. "Wondering whether you've seen them around lately."

"Ballenger and Richardson?" he asked.

"You came up with that quickly."

"They've missed strength and conditioning training for several days. If it were baseball season, I'd be really upset."

"Maybe upset isn't a bad idea. You have any clue where they might be?"

"What's this about?" he asked.

"Is your third-string shortstop any good?"

"I don't even have a third string...wait. You're saying they...they might not be back?"

I took a seat across from him. "Based on the information I learned earlier today, the police are going to be very interested in talking with them. Detective Crymes of the Pacifica Police Department tried to interview Ballenger the other day, but he wasn't home. Hasn't been for over a week."

"Pacifica," he repeated. "This is about Brandon Hunt?"

"You're quick," I said.

"Wasn't quick enough for The Show, sad to say."

"Many are called. Few are chosen. Yeah. It's about Hunt. But Detective Crymes is handling the murder investigation. I'm working on something else. What can you tell me about Richardson and Ballenger? I know they're competitive."

"Competitive ain't the word. You know they got into a fight over the shortstop position?"

"I know they say they did. I also talked with them about a month ago, and they looked thick as thieves."

"Kids," he said, waving his hand in the air. "What do they know? Both guys are sophomores. They're nineteen. Their brains are still cooking. These kids throw down one day and hang together the next."

"You observed them after the fight?"

"Yeah. They showed up for training, regular like always. I saw the scabs and bruises on their hands. Brought them into my office for a *Come To Jesus* talk. They told me all about the fight. I saw to it they buried the hatchet before they walked out the door. Probably why they were so friendly when you talked with them. How are they connected to Hunt?"

"Has either of them ever mentioned him?" I asked. "Did they talk about him at all?"

"Sure," Lee said. "Tony can't stand him."

"So why did he take Hunt's class?"

"The course is what we call a *plum*. Every department has them—courses that are incredibly popular but are only offered for one or two sections a year. For majors in those subjects, if you don't get into one of those sections, you got no hair on your balls, know what I mean? It looks bad on your transcript."

"And Hunt's forensic psych course is one of those, I suppose. He told me it's only offered once a year."

"So Tony had to register for it when it was available. Despite Hunt's widespread reputation, Tony thought it would be a smooth ride. Told me he'd sit in the back and hold his tongue. He wasn't ready for the shit Hunt spewed."

"I take it you weren't a fan."

"I don't care about him, personally, one way or the other. We didn't travel in the same circles. Barely knew the guy. Some of the stuff he believed, though...Well, I don't think we'd get along."

"And now that he's silenced?" I asked.

"I haven't wasted any tears on him, if that's what you mean. I was kind of surprised to hear he was dead. If you think people hated him when he was a professor, how do you think they felt when he was booted from the university and started making money hand-over-fist as a fringe media darling? The rage factor went up three hundred percent in the faculty meetings. Someone suggested hiring him back just so we could shut him up a little."

"Didn't work the first time."

"Anyway, he fell in shit and came up smelling of roses. He was rolling in cash. Who does themselves in when they have it made in the shade?"

"Some people like to go out on top. The word around campus is he killed himself?"

"Didn't he? Way I heard it, they found him trussed up in leather with a plastic bag over his head. Some kind of asphyxiation kink. Doesn't make much sense to me, but different strokes for different folks, right?"

"I believe you just quoted the San Francisco City Charter. Where did you hear about Hunt?"

He shrugged. "Beats me. General gossip. Day after somebody found him. That wasn't you, was it?"

"No."

"Seems like the next day everyone knew about the way he was found. I overheard some folks laughing about it before a faculty meeting. Guy like Hunt, going out tied up like a rodeo calf with a bag over his head and a butt plug up his ass. I suppose we should have some reverence for the dead, but sometimes you just gotta laugh at the way nature levels the scales."

"So Tony had a beef with Hunt?" I already knew he did. I saw the live show in Hunt's classroom.

"Are you asking if he might have done something to Hunt? Is this about that beatdown Hunt got a week or so before he was fired? You think Tony did that? And Mark?"

"Do you?" I asked.

"But the fight at the frat house—"

"I checked. There was plenty of time to get from the field house to the party after the assault. Mark and Tony easily could have attacked Hunt and dashed back to the house to stage their only alibi. I have a witness who told me they did it, along with at least one other kid and maybe more. Now, Hunt's dead, and nobody has seen either kid for over a week. So, I'll ask you again. Do you think Tony and Mark were capable of pulling something like that off?"

Lee looked as if I'd ripped out his heart. "I want to say no, Mr. Gold. I really do. But these are kids. Who in hell knows what they're capable of? I don't want to believe it about Tony. Ballenger is going to be fine. His family has connections. Tony? The kid has plans, Mr. Gold. He wants to go somewhere that doesn't involve years of bus rides between podunk towns to play Single-A ball in some high school stadium. He has the drive and the potential to go somewhere big."

"Let's just hope it isn't a penitentiary," I said.

FORTY-TWO

I pulled out my phone as I left the sports complex. Crymes answered on the second ring.

"Ballenger and Richardson were in on the attack on Hunt," I said. "So was the Plyler kid. Dean opted out."

"But he knew about it?"

"He heard the others talking about it. He said it sounded like a bad idea, so he told them to leave him out. I just talked with the baseball coach. Richardson and Ballenger haven't shown up for training in over a week. So we have four missing conspirators."

"Conspirators? That's a huge jump, Gold."

"In the assault. Maybe the murder, too, but I know that Plyler, Richardson, and Ballenger attacked Hunt, and I think Amy Popowicz was in on it as well. There's more, though. Except for Popowicz, all the kids involved in the assault are majoring in psychology."

"Intriguing."

"If you check, I bet you'll find out they all took Hunt's courses at one time or another."

"I'll access those records today. You think this entire thing is about getting even with a teacher?"

"I've seen people killed for less," I said. "Um...You didn't tell me about the butt plug."

"What butt plug?" Crymes asked. I could hear the lie in his voice.

"The baseball coach just described Hunt's precise condition when he was found at the beach shack. Exactly what have you released to the press?"

"Nothing. Hunt's dead. That's it. There's a lid on the rest."

"Not anymore. According to the coach, half the faculty knew how he was found the next day. I bet, if you do a web search on it, the description is already out there."

"Shit," he said, after a short silence.

"A butt plug? Really?"

"I don't have to share everything with you, Gold. You're saying I have a leak in my department?"

"Maybe not. If I'm right, besides your crew, there are at least four people who know how Hunt was dumped."

"Because they dumped him," Crymes said.

"Maybe one of them passed the word around. It makes sense. From your description, whoever moved the body posed Hunt in the most humiliating position possible. It was the final insult. What better way to kick the guy when he's doing the big down and out, than to ensure the final image the world saw of him would be completely degrading. By spreading the word, they maximize the public exposure. They burned the fields and salted the earth."

"Sounds like a hell of a grudge," Crymes said.

"Like half the murders we've ever seen."

"True enough. I'll put together a BOLO on our four missing kids. Maybe one of them will come up for air and we'll get a line on them."

"I'm meeting with the chief of campus security tomorrow morning," I said. "If I learn anything useful, I'll let you know right away."

I had just pocketed my phone when someone called me from behind.

"Eamon!"

I turned to find Earleen Marley. "Are you following me, Professor?" I asked.

"Heading to my car. Blew off my office hours today. Thought I'd head home and primp a little before tonight."

"Right. You and Sonny. How's that going?"

"You know that scene in *Young Frankenstein*? Madeline Kahn singing *Oh, sweet mystery of life?*"

"Sure."

"I pity the bitch."

"That good?"

"Sonny's so sweet. At first glance, he looks like someone should be minding him with a whip and a chair. But the boy is polite and courteous, and he knows how to treat a modern woman. If I were the commitment type, I could really fall for him. I'm not looking for Mr. Right, but he makes the perfect Mr. Right Now."

"Careful. That's how Heidi and I started. Change of subject?"

"Sure."

"Tell me everything you know about the nineteen year old brain in thirty seconds."

"Okay. It's immature, especially in the higher functioning areas of the prefrontal cortex. That's where we live—that is, our conscious, self-aware thinking selves. Most other stuff is autonomic, but in the prefrontal cortex we do all the stuff that makes us *us.*"

"And that part is still cooking at nineteen."

"Colorful metaphor."

"I stole it from a baseball coach."

"Marvin has a colorful way of expressing himself. But yes. The prefrontal cortex doesn't really concretize until the early to middle twenties. Like personality, it's fluid and malleable throughout the adolescent years. The closer one gets to the twenties, the more mature the brain becomes, but at nineteen there's still a long way to go in critical thinking and appropriate decision making."

"They make bad decisions?"

"Tons of them. There's a reason STDs are epidemic on college campuses. While the reasoning part of the brain is developing, most decision making comes under the purview of a lower region of the brain called the limbic system, the seat of all our emotions. They do things because they want to. Emotion is at the base of every choice. If it feels good, do it."

"Teenagers are hedonists."

"They're hormones in sneakers, Eamon. They're driven by their glands, not by reason. Why do you ask?"

"Trying to understand. If I do, it seems that nineteen year olds are more likely to act impulsively, without considering the consequences down the road."

"You were a cop," she said. "You walked a beat."

"Sure."

"Was a kid with a gun the scariest thing you could run across?"

"Unless Godzilla was in town."

"Because you could reason with an adult. A kid? There's no predicting what they'll do."

FORTY-THREE

Sandy Dennis had told me she was working as a research assistant in Dr. Friedman's cognitive processes lab in the psychology department. I found it on the third floor of the building.

When I hear the word *laboratory*, I think of a place full of Bunsen burners and Erlenmeyer flasks. A psych lab is a different animal. In this case, it was an alcove waiting area with three doors and a sullen coed sitting at a reception desk. The chairs were hard plastic. I showed the kid at the desk my card and told her I needed to talk with Sandy Dennis. She popped a gum bubble and wrote my name on a roster.

"Be about ten minutes," she said, and turned back to a textbook opened on the desktop.

It took twelve, but I wasn't really in a hurry. The door opened, and Sandy escorted another coed from her office. They laughed at something one of them had said before opening the door. Sandy placed a hand on the other woman's shoulder and wished her well. Then Sandy saw me. Her face clouded.

"Oh, shit," she said. "Believe me. I didn't do it. I don't know who did."

"Jumping a little ahead in the conversation," I said, as I stood up. "How about we start with *hello*."

"Come back to my office," she said, and turned to the receptionist. "Reschedule my next subject. I need a few minutes to talk with Mr. Gold."

Sandy's office was spartan, befitting her lowly status as a student research assistant. The desk was utilitarian pressed sawdust covered with photographed wood grain, and it offended my esthetic as a master woodworker. The chair had squeaky wheels and made a metallic grinding sound when she swiveled. The only other piece of furniture was a faded orange cloth loveseat that had obviously been college property since I was a student. Sandy had tried to personalize the space with a couple of thrift store pictures on the wall and a plant in the windowsill. Her desktop was scattered with papers, surveys, and questionnaires. A pile of folders sat next to a two-year old desk calendar.

She gestured toward the loveseat as she shut the door.

"For what it's worth, I believe you," I said.

"Why?" she said, taking a seat at her desk.

"You aren't missing, for one thing. Every other suspect on my list has gone to ground."

"So I was a suspect?" she asked.

I held my thumb and index finger a centimeter apart. "A minor one. I have an active imagination. I could see several ways you could fit in. But here you are, and here they ain't. That means something."

"Wait," she said. "Missing? You mean, like disappeared?"

"This is the first you've heard about this? Doctor Friedman is Earleen Marley's research partner, right?"

"Yes."

"Tony Richardson is one of his research assistants. You must know him."

She smiled. "Of course I do." It took her that long to process my meaning. "Tony's missing?"

"For about a week. You haven't noticed?"

"Tony isn't working on this project. Doctor Friedman has two or three studies going on right now. What happened to him?"

"That's what I'm trying to find out. Let's go back a little, though. What you said in the waiting room. It sounded like you thought I was here to nail you for Hunt's murder."

"I did," she said.

"So you think he was murdered?"

"You don't?"

"You've heard the rumors about how he was found?"

"Sure. Half the faculty thinks he pulled his own pin."

"Not you," I said.

"It doesn't play. I told you before, people didn't understand Hunt. He was seventy percent show. He enjoyed riling people up. He said that was the only way to make them think. I saw through all that. There was a lot to Brandon that people just didn't get."

"He called you *a half-breed mongrel slut.*"

I felt awful telling her. But I needed her to live in the real world for at least a few minutes. Her scowl was immediate. Tears welled up in her eyes, and she reached for a tissue.

"Why in hell would you tell me something like that?" She dabbed at her eyes.

"Makes you think, huh?" I said. "I'm not trying to drag you over the hurdles, here. I'm just trying to find some answers, and for some reason you have a huge blind spot when it comes to Hunt that's getting in the way. Before he died, Hunt told me he confronted you about the blackmail."

"Yeah. Showed up at my front door. He was drunk and high. Made a lot of accusations. I told him to pound sand, or I'd call the cops."

"But *I'm* the one who doesn't get Hunt?"

"You've made your point, Mr. Gold."

"Tony and a bunch of his buds are in big trouble right now. You think someone murdered Hunt? So do I. But that's a police case, so I have to stay away from it. Fortunately, if I'm right, the blackmail case intersects with the murder. I'm working my end of it. You were blackmailed too. What happened in the end?"

"Nothing," she said. "I rolled the dice. Didn't pay up. If the pictures are out there, they've been swallowed up by the deluge of porn on the web. Maybe I'm not important enough to draw any attention. Or they never released them at all. Either way, I sweated enough when the pictures of Hunt and me hit the porn sites. Nobody has recognized me in those yet. Thank god for that fucking purple wig."

"I thought you wanted to be famous."

"Sometimes things seem like a good idea at first. Later?" She shrugged her shoulders.

"Have you heard from Amy Beth Popowicz again?"

"Who? Is she some reporter?"

That clinched it. Either Sandy Dennis was the coolest customer I'd ever interviewed, or she was just a minor player in the Hunt tragedy. If she were part of the crew who might have put Hunt's lights out, she probably would have slipped when I dropped Amy Beth out of the blue. I was satisfied that Sandy wasn't involved.

"You knew her as Mandy," I said.

"The blonde!" she said.

"Her name is Amy Beth Popowicz. She's mixed up somehow with Tony and another couple of psych majors named Mark Ballenger and Phil Plyler."

"I know all those guys. And, I guess if you get right down to it, I know Amy Beth as well. Just not by that name. All of them are suspects?"

"Tony and Amy Beth are buddies. Tony, Mark, and Phil were in on the attack on Hunt. That's a fact. Tony and Mark fought at a frat kegger later that night over Amy Beth Popowicz."

"Too many coincidences," she said.

"If I'm right, Amy Beth ran an extortion scam on Hunt with the guys. She's an actress. When I interviewed her, she appeared completely surprised to learn the guy in the pictures was Hunt. She was throwing shade. I think she recognized him the night she came to your house, and she stole the pictures from your phone and hatched a plan to get rid of Hunt. Worse, I think Tony Richardson tipped her off, and she knew what she was walking into when my partner and I interviewed her. She had plenty of time to get into her dumb blonde character."

"I can tell you she knew who Hunt was. I introduced him, and she recognized him. Why would she want to get rid of him?"

"She's in thick with Tony Richardson. Tony hated Hunt's guts. Maybe it rubbed off."

"Sure. I can see that. Social facilitation. Cognitive dissonance. Groupthink. I can think of several psychological explanations."

"You're just an undergrad?" I asked.

"An exceptionally talented undergrad," she said.

"So, I need you to tell me the truth. The night you chose Amy Beth—Mandy—on the dating app, you'd never met or seen her before?"

"I can't say for sure. I might have seen her on campus, but we definitely didn't know each other. I was attracted to her, and so was Brandon, so we selected her."

"And this was the first time she met Hunt?"

"As far as I know."

I leaned back on the loveseat. It creaked ominously. "It was all just dumb lousy luck," I said.

"Come again?"

"You could have picked any of a hundred different women that night. By random chance, you picked one who was wired in with a kid who hated Hunt more than a chronic toothache. She's an actress. She can pretend to be anything, do anything, and see it as just acting. The sex was pretend for her. Even as Hunt was putting it to her, she was thinking about how to turn it to her advantage. After you all fell asleep, she cadged the pictures from your phone. She took it back to Tony, and they decided this was the way to get rid of Hunt for good."

"Blackmail him into resigning," Sandy said.

"But it didn't work. So Tony recruited a few other psych majors who also held grudges against Hunt, and they attacked him as he walked to his car. Then Tony and Mark Ballenger made their way back to Ballenger's frat house and staged a fight over Amy Beth."

"And Brandon still didn't resign," she said.

"So they released the pictures. You were never really in danger. I think they blackmailed you to keep you quiet."

"Fat chance."

I was growing to like Sandy Dennis. She was bright and perceptive. Could make a good detective someday. Could make a good anything someday, for that matter. Even as the thought crossed my mind, her face grew dark.

"Wait," she said. "That means...Mr. Gold, am I responsible for Brandon's murder?"

"No," I said.

"But I brought Mandy, or Amy Beth, or whatever she's calling herself this week into his life. You *do* believe she and Tony killed him, don't you?"

"What makes you say that?"

"It's the logical conclusion. There are no other viable suspects."

"Even if that's right, that doesn't make *you* responsible," I said. "You had no intent to harm Hunt. The cards just broke bad. It happens. You should prepare yourself. If Amy Beth and Tony and their buddies killed Hunt, you're going to be forced to testify. That purple wig isn't going to protect your anonymity on the stand. Hate to tell you, kid, but you might get famous after all."

FORTY-FOUR

Sonny fell back against the pillows, sweating and breathing heavily. He wasn't gasping. Sonny never gasped, under any circumstances. But he was confident Earleen had just taken his breath away. Earleen fell across his chest and didn't bother pulling the sheets up to cover them. Her body crushed against his as she craned her neck to kiss him.

"Damn," he said. "Just...damn."

"You are completely welcome," she said, kissing him again, just a light peck. "I'm impressed as well. You have the job."

He pulled her even closer and wrapped his arms around her.

They were in Sonny's condo, with its panoramic view of the bay. The Golden Gate Bridge was brightly illuminated, a ginger ribbon spanning the water to Mount Tam and Marin County. Fog crept over the mountain, spilling down toward the giant redwood spires of Muir Woods and the bridge. Within minutes, the bridge would be engulfed, and in an hour the entire city would lie under a thick blanket of mist.

Earleen sighed. "Is this a great city or what?"

"Don't let it hear you," Sonny whispered. "It's already got a big head."

He reached for the bottle of Krug Brut on the nightstand and freshened their glasses. He held both up while Earleen rolled over to sit against the pillows, and then handed her one. Without any verbal salute, they clinked the glasses and sipped.

"Are you like this every time you close a case?" she asked. "Because I like it. I selfishly wish you boatloads of success in the detective game."

"I closed it, I guess," he said. "Don't know if it was a success."

"If the check clears, it's a success."

"Wish I felt that way. But let's not talk about that. It's kind of a downer, and I feel too good to get sucked back into that morass."

"Morass," she said. "Eloquent, too."

"I was an English major," he said. "Vocabulary's kinda my thing."

"Here's to not winning them all, then." She raised her glass, and they clinked once again. "Eamon came by my office today. Did he tell you?"

"No."

"He's still working the Brandon Hunt case."

"Says he's not done yet," Sonny said. "Doesn't think he gave Hunt his money's worth. Now that Hunt's dead, Eamon wants to fill in all the blanks. He's strange that way. Nobody probably cares about it now that the pictures are out, and Hunt's been murdered."

"Murdered?" she asked. "The rumor in the halls was he committed suicide."

"Oh, boy," he said. "Too much champagne. Forget I said it. Seriously. The last thing I need is that Detective Crymes from Pacifica to come down around my head."

"But Eamon's not working on the murder case."

"See? There you go again. Ixnay on the urdermay, okay? No. He's wrapping up some details from the time we were working for Hunt. Tying up all the loose ends. Really, that's all I know. Want some more?" He hefted the bottle.

"Hit me."

He alternated pouring between glasses, to make sure they both got the same amount from the remainder of the bottle. "Another dead soldier," he said, dropping the bottle back into the ice bin. "We're laying waste to the enemy tonight."

She sipped a couple of times, taking a few breaths to savor it. "He said some of my students are involved."

"Who?"

"Eamon. This afternoon. He mentioned Tony Richardson and Mark Ballenger and Phil Plyler."

Sonny placed the glass on the bedside table and turned back to her.

"Ask your questions," he said.

"You're upset?"

"No. But it's obvious you're curious, and if you're thinking about that, you aren't thinking about this. So let's take it off the table and get back to checking for moles."

"Let's start with Brandon. He was murdered? For real?"

"Crymes is treating it that way."

"Why do they think that?"

Sonny took another sip of the champagne. "He was moved after death, and he didn't die at his beach shack. The four kids who blackmailed and assaulted Hunt are in the wind. That looks very suspicious. Tox screen will come back soon, and I'm betting it will show he was doped before he was bagged. And that, literally, is everything I know about it."

"Extrapolate from that," she said.

"Extrapolate," he repeated. "That may be the first time a naked woman has ever said that word to me. It might be the first time any naked woman has said it at all."

"I'm a scientist," she whispered, as she kissed his cheek. "Occupational hazard. And I will understand completely if you bring a magnifying glass to bed. Seriously. From what you know, what do you think happened?"

"I think your students have been extremely naughty. The pictures of Hunt released to the public showed him with two students. One of them is in your department."

"Sandy," she said. "I know. Recognized her immediately. We haven't talked about it, though. Awkward, right?"

"The other woman in the picture is tight with Tony Richardson." He explained how they had blackmailed Hunt, and then kicked the shit out of him when he didn't respond immediately, and finally how they released the pictures to follow through on their threats. "Now they've vanished, and Hunt is dead. Best guess? They killed him and split in four directions."

"I can't buy that," Earleen said. "I know these kids, Sonny. And they *are* kids. I just don't see them doing something so vicious."

"We already have a witness who says Tony, Mark, and Phil were in on the assault. The other evidence looks very bad for them and this Amy Beth chick in the picture."

"Amy Beth Popowicz?"

He sat upright. "You know her?"

"She was a student in my Intro course. She's the girl in the pictures?"

"Yeah."

"Jesus. I introduced her to Tony. They met in my class. This is too weird."

"We'll get final proof tomorrow," he said. "At least on the extortion. Eamon traced the blackmail note to a specific printer on campus, and there's a security camera looking right at it. We know when it was printed, so he's checking the security footage tomorrow afternoon. I'm betting either Tony or Amy Beth will pick it out of the printer."

Earleen drained her glass and placed it on the bedside table, then rolled over and burrowed into his chest. "Sonny, there's something—"

Sonny's phone buzzed on the nightstand. The screen read *Eamon.*

"Yeah," Sonny said.

"Turn on your TV."

"Which channel?"

"Any of them."

Sonny glanced at the clock. Eleven-oh-one. He grabbed the remote and turned on the flatscreen in the bedroom. A local reporter stood in the fog outside a familiar house in Mill Valley. The graphic running across the bottom of the screen read *Murder-Suicide in Affluent Marin County Neighborhood.* Sonny thumbed up the volume as an on-scene reporter began to speak.

The words tumbled around Sonny's ears. *Signs of a violent argument. Bypassers reported several gunshots. Two dead. One gun. Neighbors in shock. Alan Standish, sixty-two, noted San Francisco attorney and polo enthusiast. Isabel Standish, forty-eight, art aficionado and philanthropist.*

"Oh fuck," Sonny said. "Oh, Jesus. What the fuck, Eamon?"

"You need to get your ass in gear. I got a five-minute head's up from the Mill Valley PD. Some detective named Turlock. Want to bet his nickname's *Sherlock?*"

"No time for jokes."

"He wants to parlay. You ever been interrogated?"

"Only in military training. Never for real."

"Welcome to the club, rookie. Two rules. The nice guy on the other side of the table is not your friend. The days of rubber hoses and rolled up phone books are long gone. They use something called the Reid Method now. Sweet cop sweeter cop stuff. Some of these guys will put cavities in your teeth. Don't fall for it. You are not there to make new buddies. Rule Two. Tell the absolute truth, but as little of it as possible. Keep your answers to as few words as you can. They'll use silence to sucker you into talking. Don't fall for it. Answer the question, and then shut up and wait for them to ask another one. If you feel threatened at any point, ask for an attorney. I'm texting you the name of mine, and I'm telling him to expect your call."

Sonny stood and crossed to the window, gazing out toward the bridge. "Okay. Understood. Thanks."

"You okay, partner?"

"Gotta tell you, Eamon, I'm kinda freakin' out here."

"Tell the cops what you told Standish, and you'll be fine. Piece of cake."

"No. I mean, my client *died,* man."

"Small world. That's not on you, Sonny. Remember what we talked about. You played him straight. He was the crooked one. That's out of your control. You need to get dressed and scoot down to the office. The detective from Mill Valley is headed this way to take your statement. Play him right, and maybe you can avoid riding over the bridge tonight. This is part of the game. Don't sweat it."

Sonny put the phone down. It immediately buzzed again. *Jack Delroy.*

"Malehala."

On the other end, Delroy sounded half-drunk. "What in hell did you tell Standish!"

"You're sauced."

"Getting there. Answer the question."

"He was my client. I told him the truth. Isabel hired you. She was having an affair with Weber, who tossed him to the state bureau. Charges were imminent, to be followed closely by divorce papers. I also told him I knew all this from you, and that I had no direct physical evidence. He terminated my services. End of story."

"Jesus!" Delroy spat. "What a clusterfuck. Do you have any idea what it's like going after an estate for payment?"

"Should have taken your own advice, Jack. I deposited his check today."

"Got a silver Eisenhower dollar in my pocket says they freeze payment on the check. Police are probably locking down his accounts as we speak. Ain't either of us gonna get paid on this gig, amigo."

"Gotta boogie. Is there some point to this call?"

"Weber's out of pocket."

"Sober up a little and say that again," Sonny said.

"Soon's I heard from Moon that cops were headed up to the Standish place, I checked in on Weber. He was gone. Maybe he got spooked or something, but I have no idea where he is. I got a statey breathing down my neck right now. My phone blistered my hand last time he called. Just wanted to touch base so you know, no matter how bad you got it tonight, someone's taking it up the chute worse."

"Sorry the chips fell that way," Sonny said.

"Yeah. Fuck you back. See me on the street? Cross to the other side."

"We're cool, brother."

"Fuck off."

Sonny turned to find Earleen sitting up in bed, the sheets gathered under her neck, staring at him.

"This is what you do?" she asked.

"It is tonight. Sorry. I gotta go."

"I heard. Your phone's kinda loud. I'll get dressed."

Sonny exited the bathroom after starting the shower. "No need. I can't say when I'll get back tonight, though. Might have to cross the bridge."

"Don't worry about it. I have stuff to do at home anyway. Like sleep."

He took her hand. "Come on. Shower's running. I hear police detectives give breaks to guys with really clean backs."

FORTY-FIVE

I met Sonny for breakfast the next morning. He looked like he'd ridden bareback over ten miles of cobblestones, but at least he wasn't in irons.

"How'd it go with Sherlock Turlock?" I asked.

Sonny sipped at his coffee. "Wasn't him. Apparently, Turlock is the chief of detectives up in Mill Valley."

"How many detectives do they need?" I said. "You could fit the population of Mill Valley into a high school gym."

"The guy I talked with was named Bludis. Jack Bludis. Older fellow. Close to retirement, but he knew his shit. His interrogation was a work of art."

"And yet, being full of grace, here you are."

Sonny buttered a slice of toast and then smeared some mixed fruit preserves on it. "It was straightforward. From what I can gather from the subtext, Isabel got pissed that Alan had hired a detective to spy on her, and when she confronted him, he confronted her right back. One of the last things Standish said to me was *the bitch won*. He was obsessed with the idea he might go to jail and she'd go on as before, albeit hoisted on the petard of her new boytoy."

"Ouch," I said.

"Standish was desperate. He had already lost, but he couldn't let her win."

"Like I said. Half our cases are zero sum games. Standish was going to hire someone, Sonny. Sooner or later, he and Isabel were destined to go to the mattresses, and not in a good way. What about Weber?"

"That's the best part. He's disappeared."

"Seems to be a growth industry these days."

"Still no sign of Amy Beth and the Rover Boys?" Sonny asked.

"They're dug in deep. Crymes tried to ping their cell phones. Got nothing. Probably running on drugstore burners."

"Or maybe they're under a couple feet of dirt," Sonny said, just as the waitress arrived to freshen his coffee cup. She glanced at him, her face concerned, and turned to walk away.

"Whatever, they're dark. I have a meeting with Chief Couchell after lunch. We'll check the security videos, and I'll wrap up the blackmail case, at least. Maybe it will help find who killed Hunt, but that's Crymes' business. Did this Bludis guy say anything about talking with you again?"

"The usual. Don't leave town, blah blah blah. Boilerplate stuff. I gave him Standish's motive. He's probably satisfied. I might have to testify at the inquest, but that will be the end of it."

"Good. Go get some sleep. You look like you need it."

———

Chief Couchell greeted me himself as I walked through the Campus Police office door. He stood about two inches shorter than me, and his tight curly hair was shot through with strands of gray. I put him around fifty, but the bags under his eyes might have added a year or two. His voice sounded like he smoked two packs a day.

"Expected you over a month ago," he said.

"I appreciate you seeing me today. Brandon Hunt hired me to help protect him after the assault near the field house. In the course of performing that job, he confided in me that he was being blackmailed."

"The pictures that got released," Couchell said. "That's what they had on him?"

"The girls in the pictures were coeds. Taboo. I think one of them was blackmailing him. I can also wrap up your assault case. I have the names of three students who were in on it. There may have been more." I gave him the names, which he wrote on a pocket notepad.

"I've got missing person reports on all these kids," he said.

"That's what worries me. They all went missing the day Hunt died."

I could tell he immediately caught my meaning.

"How can we help?" he asked.

"I know when and where the blackmail note was printed. It was the computer lab in the student center. There are security cameras in the area. I'm hoping one of them caught the person who picked up the printout."

"And you want to check the security videos."

"It will tell me for sure if students were involved. It might help explain why Hunt was murdered as well."

"Let's get to it, then," he said.

Minutes later, we were in a stifling control room, sitting before a panel of computer screens. Couchell sat at a console. I backed up my chair for a better view of the screens.

"Back in the day," he said, as he tapped at a keyboard, "this shit was all on videotape. Took hours to review a single reel. Now, it's all digital. I'm calling up the records of all the security cameras with a view of the computer lab. Then I just ask to see a specific time, and... *voila.*"

Four of the screens froze on different images of the lab. The videos were high resolution, so I was able to clearly see all the tables.

"This is the time the note was printed," I said, looking at the stamp on the video. "It was the middle printer on that table. Let's see who picks it up."

He zoomed the image in, so that we could focus only on that printer. It took a few seconds, but a figure appeared next to the printer and slipped the paper into a folder.

"I knew it!" I said. "Chief, that woman is Amy Beth Popowicz."

"Another missing person," he said.

"She's also the blonde in the pictures that got Hunt fired. This ties the assault into the blackmail."

"And the murder?"

"Possibly. There are no other suspects at this time."

We watched the video advance, as Amy Beth walked calmly to the door and out into the student center commons.

She headed directly for the food court. She stopped and scanned the crowd. A look of recognition appeared on her face, and she waved briefly before walking out of the frame.

"Looks like she's meeting someone in the food court," I said. "Do you have any cameras covering that area?"

"This is a university. We have cameras everywhere. Hold on."

He made a note of the time stamp and pulled up several more camera files. The view switched to a reverse of the previous camera. Now we saw Amy Beth's back as she exited the lab. She again crossed toward the food court, hesitated, and waved. We watched as she waded among the tables and trash cans, until she stopped beside one of the many planters used for room dividers, to offer the semblance of privacy. She appeared to talk to someone sitting behind the divider, and then handed over the folder with the printout before walking away.

"Can't see who that is," Couchell said.

"Wait a second," I told him. Sure enough, after a few seconds, the figure behind the divider stood and walked around, facing directly into the security camera.

I gasped. "Holy shit," I said. "Well. I never saw that coming."

FORTY-SIX

Sonny awakened from a sound sleep, roused by the buzzing of his cellphone. He didn't even look at the screen before answering, because that would have required opening his eyes.

"What?"

"Is Earleen with you?" It was Eamon.

"I wish. She's at work, man."

"No. She isn't. Chief Couchell checked, and she phoned in sick today. I just went by her apartment. Nobody answered the door."

"What in hell time is it?" Sonny asked.

"Almost four-thirty. We've been looking all over for her."

Sonny sat up in bed, suddenly wide awake. "What's happened?"

"I hate laying heavies on you like this, partner, but we have a big problem."

"Is Earleen okay?" Sonny said. "Is she in danger?"

"Shower and get dressed. I'm on the way over."

"Damn it, Eamon. Tell me now."

"As far as I know, she's okay. It's too complicated to explain on the phone. I'm on the way."

Sonny turned on the shower, and then dialed Earleen on his cell. The phone rang a few times and went to voicemail. "This is Sonny. I need to talk to you. Call me as soon as you get this message." He beat the beep by a half-second. To emphasize the call-back, he texted her as well.

He had just finished dressing when Eamon knocked on the door. Sonny opened it, and Eamon charged in.

"I missed it entirely," he said, without even a greeting. "Everyone but Amy Beth was a psych major, and they all worked either for Earleen or her partner."

"What are you talking about?"

Sonny saw a new emotion cross his partner's face. He couldn't tell for sure, but it looked like pity.

"Sit down."

Sonny took a seat. Eamon hovered over him, pacing, and moving his hands as he spoke.

"I hate to break it to you, man, but we've been played. Earleen was involved in the blackmail scheme, which also implicates her in the assault and the murder."

"I don't believe you," Sonny said.

"Doesn't matter. Facts are facts. Couchell and I watched the videos this afternoon. Amy Beth printed out the blackmail note and picked it up. Minutes later, she passed it to Earleen in the food court. I didn't think you'd believe me, so I had Couchell print out screen captures."

He pulled an envelope from his jacket and handed it to Sonny. Inside were several stills from the surveillance video.

Amy Beth at the printer, putting a sheet of paper into a folder. Amy Beth in the food court, handing the folder to an unseen person behind the divider. Earleen Marley walking into the frame, still holding the folder and facing the camera.

"I already forwarded this information to Detective Crymes," Eamon said. "I probably should have called you first, but as soon as we found out Earleen called in sick, we had to move fast. You were with her last night?"

"Yeah," Sonny said, looking two sizes too small for his clothes.

"Did you talk about the case?"

"I fucked up. I let it slip that Crymes was investigating Hunt's death as a murder. I told her to forget I said it, but of course she couldn't. Maybe she was involved in the extortion, but that doesn't mean she was in on the murder."

Eamon stared at him.

"Does it?" Sonny demanded.

"How did she react when you told her?"

Sonny tried to recall. "She...she didn't seem shocked. A little surprised, perhaps. She kept asking questions about the case. Mostly, she seemed concerned about her students. She remembered Amy Beth. According to her, Amy and Tony met in her class, when Tony was an assistant."

"How much did you tell her?"

Sonny shook his head. "Almost nothing. I did say that Richardson, Ballenger, and Plyler were all missing, and that Crymes wanted to find them, because they were his only suspects in the Hunt killing."

"Damn it, Sonny—" Eamon crossed to the window and stared out at the bay. The sun was settling into the sea, almost transecting the Golden Gate Bridge. After a few seconds, he turned back around. "Forget that. I didn't mean to jump in your shit. I'm mostly angry at myself. If I had met with Couchell a month ago, when I planned, Hunt would still be alive, and we'd have closed the case. I fucked up when he was fired, and I let the case drop."

"He fired you."

"I had time to wrap stuff up before I met with him to collect the check. I squandered it. And ignore what I said. I tell Heidi all sorts of shit I shouldn't. In this business, we need to talk to someone once in a while or we'll go crazy. Have you tried contacting Earleen?"

Sonny held up his phone. "Voice and text. Nothing."

"I'm not surprised," Eamon said. "Crymes tried to ping her phone. It's turned off."

"Just like the kids," Sonny said.

"You think she's with them?"

"I don't have a clue. I'm still trying to wrap my head around the way she played me. She was here just a few hours ago, and I didn't see a thing."

"She's a psychologist, and a damned good one. One of the best. She's an expert at manipulating people's heads."

"But... *why?*" Sonny asked. "Why blackmail Hunt in the first place, and why kill him?"

"Did she tell you about her and Hunt?" Eamon asked.

"What?"

"Man, this is not your day. They slept together, a long time back, before Hunt was tenured. She did not refer to the experience in glowing terms. She recognized Sandy Dennis in the photos. Sandy interns with Earleen's research partner, Doctor Friedman. She lied to me about only recalling Amy Beth from a class a few semesters ago. The pictures prove that. She knew all along it was Amy Beth in the pictures. But, maybe, Hunt knocking boots with one of her students drove her over the edge."

"What can I do?" Sonny asked.

"First of all, keep trying to get her on the phone. Blow up her inbox. I need you to set up a stakeout at her apartment. Maybe she didn't have time to collect her stuff before running. She's probably too smart to go for it herself, but she might send someone else. That person might lead us to Earleen. I'm going to Pacifica to brief Crymes in person."

Sonny leaned forward, bracing his hands against his knees, staring at the carpet. Eamon put a hand on his shoulder.

"I know you're hurting, brother," he said. "You trusted her, and you got burned. That's the worst feeling there is. Worse than getting shot. Later, we'll get drunk and work our way through it. But I need you on your A game tonight. Are you up to it?"

"I understand the job," Sonny said. "Just give me the go signal."

FORTY-SEVEN

Sonny sat in his car across from Earleen's apartment. It was almost eight o'clock. The sun had set over two hours earlier, and the dependable fog from Marin County had already begun to infiltrate the bay and the city. Streetlights and stop signals acquired misty haloes, endowing them with the warm ambience of an impressionist painting. Car headlights fashioned luminous cones in the fog as they drove by. All the sounds around him were muffled by the fog. If it became much thicker, Sonny thought he might have to leave the car and hang out closer to the apartment entrance.

He still couldn't imagine how Earleen had fooled him so completely. After three tours in the Rangers, and several years as a mob bodyguard, he thought he was pretty good at sizing people up.

He wasn't so foolish as to imagine he had been falling in love. He knew too much about Earleen—and about himself—to succumb to the temptations of early infatuation and mistake them for the ever-after commitment of true love. He was too cynical to be taken in by his own glands.

He had liked her, however. A lot. She was smart, and clever, and not at all difficult to look at across a candlelit table. He had believed they were compatible. Now he wondered whether it had all been a lie she perpetrated to keep tabs on Eamon's investigation into the extortion plot.

And what was *that* all about, anyway? Hunt was a royal pain the ass, but why would she put her entire career on the line just to rid the college of him? He wasn't worth it. And then, she may have killed him? Nothing in all the conversations he had enjoyed with Earleen had ever suggested her capacity to murder. None of it made sense.

He punched her number on the cellphone again. He had tried calling her every five minutes since Eamon left. Each time, the call went to voicemail. Sonny left a message every time. This time, he was notified that her voicemail inbox was full. He punched out a quick text as well, asking her for a umpteenth time to call him, and settled the phone back onto the passenger seat.

The silence in the car became overwhelming. Sonny switched on the satellite radio, to a station that played deep album cuts from the previous century. It was innocuous noise that filled the space in the car and allowed him to think. Once again, he examined every moment he had spent with Earleen over the previous month, looking for any signs he might have missed. Nothing jumped out at him. She might have attached herself to him, initially, to spy on Eamon's investigation. But why did she stay on, long after Hunt had been fired and Eamon had abandoned the case? Perhaps Earleen wasn't the complete *femme fatale*. Perhaps there was more than simple advantage in continuing to see Sonny. He wanted to believe there was at least true affection in there somewhere.

His phone buzzed. Expecting to see Eamon's name on the screen, Sonny was shocked to read Earleen's. He grabbed the phone.

"Miss me, lover?" she asked.

"Where are you? We need to talk," Sonny said.

"I take it you know, then. That explains the forty-three messages on my phone."

"I'll come to you. Just tell me where."

"So you can turn me over to the police? Oh, lover, I don't think so. And, you know what?"

"What?"

"I've ridden in your car before. I know what it looks like. Why are you sitting in front of my apartment?"

Sonny leapt from the car and scanned the surrounding area. Visibility was cut to yards by the fog, and he couldn't see a thing outside the parking lot. He ducked back into the car.

"Waiting for you to show," he said. "Like I said. We need to talk."

"Maybe later." The screen went dead. Sonny tried to dial her back, but the call went directly to the full voicemail.

A BMW coupe rounded the corner and drove by the apartment building, headlights piercing the fog until they became flat discs of light yards in front of the grille. It stopped in front of the apartment, and the dome light came on.

Sonny had ridden in Earleen's car as well, and he recognized it as easily as she had his. She waved at him, smiling, her fingers curling individually in a cartoonish way, and the dome light was extinguished. She put the car in gear and drove off.

Sonny pursued her. He called Eamon on the Bluetooth.

"Where are you?" Sonny said.

"With Crymes, in my office."

"I'm following her."

"Putting you on speaker," Eamon said.

"Looks like she's headed for the bridge," Sonny said. "She called me, Eamon. I was sitting outside her place, and she dialed me up like it was nothing. I asked to meet, but she refused."

Crymes' voice came over the speaker. "I'm contacting SFPD for backup. Where are you right now?"

Sonny told him. "They're going to have a hard time spotting her. The fog's like a whiteout in the Rockies. I'm barely keeping up with her brake lights as it is. Ping my phone. She keeps shutting hers off. As long as I can stay on her tail, you'll know where she's heading."

He heard Crymes giving the directions to the SFPD on his phone in the background.

Eamon said, "Look, Sonny, we have a line on Tony Richardson. His cellphone lit up about an hour ago. The Pacifica police are coordinating with the Marin County Sheriff's Department to pin down his location."

"He's across the bridge?" Sonny asked.

"His phone is."

"It looks like Earleen's headed that way."

"Maybe Tony contacted her. She could be going to him. Right now, you're our only eyes on Earleen. Stay on her at all costs. Don't worry about running red lights or shit. Crymes has you covered for the duration. You may have company as soon as he gets a ping on your phone. If they blow by you and try to take her down, don't interfere. Got it?"

"They'd do that?"

"It's kind of their thing," Eamon said. "If they do, let it go down. We'll deal with the emotional shrapnel later."

"Hey," Sonny said. "We just turned onto the 101. She's definitely headed for the bridge."

"Marin County deputies will stop her at the other end, if SFPD doesn't get her on this side."

Sonny's phone vibrated and beeped. He glanced at the screen.

"Eamon, she's calling me. Do you have the ping on my phone yet?"

Crymes called out, "Almost. You don't have to hold our connection. Take the call."

"We're on the way," Eamon said. "Crymes and I will take his car."

Without saying goodbye, Sonny switched to the incoming call.

"Pull over," he said. "They know Tony's location in Marin County. They'll stop you on the other side of the bridge. This only ends one way, Earleen."

"You're so cute," she said.

"This isn't a joke."

"You're telling me? Got your recorder on you?"

Sonny slapped at his jacket pocket and felt the familiar shape of the portable digital recorder Eamon had taught him to keep there.

"Why?"

"Am I on speaker?"

"Yeah."

"Start recording."

Sonny fumbled with the recorder in the darkness of the car, until he saw the red recording light. "Okay. Recording."

"This is Doctor Earleen Marley," she said. "I confess wholly and entirely to the extortion and murder of Brandon Hunt. How's that?"

"Don't fuck around, Earleen," Sonny said.

"You want the long version? Okay. How many people did Charlie Manson actually kill?"

"If you listen to him, none."

"And none were ever tied back to him, at least as the perpetrator. But he was responsible, right?"

"History says so."

"And I'm responsible too, then. I let my resentments toward Brandon color my interactions with my students. You were right. Tony hated Brandon something awful, and he was hooking up with Amy Beth. Some of my statements might have reinforced Tony's hatred, and he pulled Amy Beth along with him. When she showed up at Sandy's place for the threesome, she didn't realize it was going to be with Hunt. Soon as she recognized him, she started planning to get him fired for screwing students."

"So the extortion was her idea."

"No. She and Tony came to my office on the Monday after she had sex with Hunt. She showed me the pictures, and said she was going to take them to the Board of Regents as evidence of Hunt violating the terms of his tenure. She didn't care that she'd be sucked along into the scandal as badly as he would, and Sandy's career might be ruined as well. Amy Beth is an actress. Probably believes there's no such thing as bad publicity. I calmed them down, and suggested they try to get Hunt to resign first."

"You came up with the blackmail scheme?" Sonny said.

"I was trying to save my students. Mostly, I was buying time. Amy Beth printed out the blackmail note in the student center and gave it to me. I sent it along with the pictures to Hunt anonymously through the campus mail. Then we waited."

"What about the assault?"

"Kids. Hard to predict. I was content to let Brandon stew for as long as it took to make the right decision, or for the kids to give up and let it go. Tony and Mark had other ideas. They wanted to soften him up a little, make him more amenable to quitting the college. I didn't know about the assault until after it happened."

"And releasing the pictures?"

"Amy Beth and Tony did that. Again, they didn't tell me before they did it."

"And now we get to the biggie," Sonny said. "Who killed Hunt?"

"I already said I did."

"Why?"

"He found out. Apparently, before Brandon was fired, Eamon gave him Tony Richardson's and Mark Ballenger's names. After he was fired, he had time to do some detecting of his own. He followed Tony and saw him come to my apartment. After Tony left, Brandon visited me. He was many things, Sonny, but he was no idiot. He figured everything out from the information you and Eamon uncovered. He accused me of orchestrating the entire extortion plot."

"Which you did," Sonny said.

"Which I did, with the intent of avoiding a much more disastrous outcome. He couldn't see that, though. He threatened to get me fired, and to go to the police over the blackmail. I was desperate. I had fallen victim to my own plan, and I couldn't see any way out other than to do away with Brandon."

"How did you do it?"

"Brandon didn't know Amy Beth was part of the scheme. I arranged for her to call him and ask to see him again. She's an amazing actress. Laid it on thick. *Oh, I had no idea who you were the last time. I didn't know you were famous! I'd love to see you again.*"

"Played to his vanity."

"It was his Achilles heel. He met with her at a cheap motel. She offered him Extasy, but it was really fentanyl. While she waited for the drugs to take effect, she played a little bondage and discipline game with him. The higher he got, the easier it was to convince him to do just about anything. Then he passed out. Amy Beth let me into the room. I smothered Brandon with the dry-cleaning bag."

"Just like that?"

"It was me or him, Sonny. There's not a lot of room in that equation for hesitation."

"And the boys carried him back to his beach shack in Pacifica and left him there."

"See? The worst they can be hit with is moving a body."

"And extortion. And assault."

"But not murder. They're going to suffer for what they've done, but nobody will hang a homicide rap around their neck. They didn't know I was going to kill him. Neither did Amy Beth. She thought I was going to take more incriminating pictures to blow up his TV career."

"You lied to them the way you lied to me."

"Yes. And I'm sorry, Sonny. You deserved better. So did they. As soon as they saw I'd killed him, and we dumped him at his beach place, I told them to scatter until I could figure out how to get away with it. Tony went to Marin County. Amy Beth is back in Los Angeles. I have no idea where Phil Plyler is, but one of the others will. I thought there might be a way out of this, but when I heard about the video security cameras, I knew Eamon would see Amy Beth handing me the printout, and he's too good a detective not to figure the rest out."

Sonny saw the first red and blue police lights in his rearview mirror.

"Can you see the cops behind me?" he asked.

"No. Fog's too thick."

"They're tracking my cellphone. Once we're on the bridge, you'll be cut off on both ends. Make it easy on yourself. Pull over and we can get you the help you need."

"There's more," she said. "And I don't have a lot of time."

Two more sets of police lights joined in the parade behind them.

"It's getting crowded behind me," Sonny said. "Please, Earleen. Stop the car."

"Soon enough. I need to clear the air between us. The thing with you? It was never about Brandon Hunt. Never. Don't ever think it was. Please."

She broke the connection.

FORTY-EIGHT

Crymes and I joined the growing procession of flashing police lights behind Sonny.

"Pull around them," I said.

"Can't. This is their turf. Right now, I'm an official visitor. Same thing goes for the Marin County boys on the other side of the bridge. This is their show now."

My cellphone rang. Sonny.

"What's the story?" I asked as soon as I punched the connection button.

"She did it. She told me everything. I have her confession on my digital recorder."

We all took the on-ramp to the Golden Gate Bridge, the rotating red and blue lights ahead shimmering in the fog.

"Did you tell her the Marin County deputies were waiting for her?" I asked.

"I don't think she's living in the real world right now," Sonny said. "But her confession fits all the facts we have. I believe her, as much as it hurts to say it. I don't think she cares what happens, as long as she has a chance to get to Tony."

"Ain't gonna happen, partner," I said.

Crymes broke in. "Marin County deputies picked Richardson up ten minutes ago. He's in custody. He had several burners on him. One of them had numbers for the other two. My department's coordinating with LAPD and Seattle. We'll have all of them in an hour."

"What do I tell her if she calls back?" Sonny said.

"The truth," I said. "If she believes there's no hope, maybe she'll give herself up."

"Holy shit!" Sonny yelped.

Over the phone, we heard the squeal of tortured tires, and the brake lights on the cruisers ahead of us all lit up like Christmas trees.

"...If she believes there's no hope, maybe she'll give herself up," Eamon said over Sonny's car speakers.

At the same instant, Earleen's brake lights came on, and her car lurched sideways as the brakes locked and the tires grabbed for traction, leaving a fifty-foot ribbon of skid marks on the bridge.

Sonny jumped on his brakes to avoid her. "Holy shit!" he exclaimed, as the rear lost traction and began to swing around. He did a full spin and half of another before his car came to rest several yards beyond hers. As soon as his car stopped spinning, Sonny jumped from the driver's seat and ran toward Earleen.

She was already out and had climbed the wall separating the road surface from the pedestrian walkway. Sonny vaulted the retaining wall just as she swung one leg over the outside railing.

"Stop, Sonny!" she yelled. "Don't come a step closer!"

They were halfway across the bridge, the point highest above the deepest part of the channel. Nobody could survive a fall from that height. Sonny froze.

"Don't do this!" he yelled. He heard the stomping clatter of brogans behind him and knew the police had surrounded them. Suddenly, the world was flooded with brilliant, diffused light from the headlamps and the officers' high-powered lanterns.

"Move away, Malehala," Crymes ordered. "Let us handle this."

"Hold on!" Sonny shouted over his shoulder.

"He's right," Earleen said. "You should go. This isn't going to be pretty."

"Don't say that!" Sonny pleaded. "We can find a way—"

"—Out of a first degree murder charge? Oh, sweetie, you just don't get it. There's nothing ahead for me but decades on a lousy mattress wearing ugly clothes and beating myself up for the choices I've made. That's not my style. I just can't do prison, darlin'. For what it's worth, I never used you until last night. I could have fallen in love with you."

"I feel the same. That's something to hold onto, right?"

She smiled, tears streaming down her face. She shook her head.

"Not enough," she said, and swung the other leg over the rail. Sonny dashed toward her, as she leaned back, holding on barely with her fingertips. She raised one hand to her face when he was scant feet away and blew him a kiss. Then she let go.

Sonny reached out for her. For the rest of his life, he would believe that, for just an instant, her fingers brushed against his. And then she was falling, silently, tumbling head over heels deep into the fog, until she disappeared completely and forever into the black yonder.

FORTY-NINE

The Golden Gate channel currents are tricky, and the bay isn't exactly the kind of place you can dredge. Earleen Marley's body never floated ashore. The best guess was she was swept out to sea. Maybe she had a secret parachute, and yanked the ripcord halfway to the water, and was picked up by a confederate in a speedboat. But I kinda doubted it.

Sonny took it hard. After hours of questioning by Crymes and then some more from the SFPD, I took him out for breakfast. He piddled with the food on his plate, pushing it around with his fork, and he said not one word the entire time except to give the waitress his order. I didn't try to engage him in conversation. What was there to say, really? It was enough for him to know I was there.

He didn't show up at the office for a few days. I didn't push it. He knew he was welcome whenever he decided to return.

Days passed into weeks. Whenever Heidi asked me where Sonny was, I just shrugged. I dropped by the Dogpatch District and the 3rd Street Gym, hoping to find him there. The head trainer told me he hadn't seen Sonny in over a month.

I checked his apartment from time to time. He was never there. When I called his cell, I was informed the number had been disconnected.

I floated through my annual downtime at Thanksgiving and Christmas. Somehow, people don't have much need for private cops around the holidays. Heidi and I spent Christmas in Jackson Hole at the Grand Tetons. We watched them drop the big crystal ball on television, and a new year rolled over us.

Amy Beth, Tony Richardson, Mark Ballenger, and Phil Plyler all drew time for extortion, assault and battery, and accessories to murder. Amy Beth's father was some kind of Hollywood studio exec. He hired a hotshot lawyer who got the murder charges dropped in return for a guilty plea on the others. It wasn't difficult, since Earleen's recorded confession clearly stated they didn't know about the murder until afterward. The kids jumped on the deal anyway. Being first offenders all, they got the minimum sentences. They'll barely miss a year of school.

Well, they'll miss a lot more than that, having been expelled from the university, which also told them *Lotsa luck getting in anywhere else.*

I walked into my office in March, and found Sonny sitting at his desk.

"You owe me back rent on the office," I said, as I hung my jacket on the coat tree next to the door.

"You know anyone bigger than me you can send to collect?" he said.

"Got me there. Thought maybe you'd gone to work for Sheldon Moon."

"Wasn't sure I wanted to work for anyone, at least doing this. Needed some time to get my shit together."

"So, what's your status, shit-wise?" I asked.

"Getting there. Thought I'd dip my toe in, see if you have anything easy on tap, like an international assassination or stopping a nuclear attack."

"Easing back in," I said. "Good idea."

We stared at each other for a bit.

"I'm fuckin' with you," he said. "Got another gig."

"That a fact? Does this have anything to do with you being completely off the grid for the last five months?"

"Did some traveling. Went to visit some family in the islands. Bopped around for a while. Drank all the mai-tais in Honolulu. Picked up a wahine or two. Put some skin between me and Earleen."

"Did it help?"

"It didn't hurt. But it didn't take away the memories, either. I just don't know if I'm cut out for this sort of thing, Eamon. I appreciate the hell out of all you've done. You saved my life, man, but you're on a trip I don't think works so well for me."

"Fair enough. It isn't for everyone. So," I said. "Tell me about this new gig."

"Hotel security?" Heidi said, after I told her what Sonny would be doing.

We were dining at Ruth's Chris, a celebration of another closed case and a fat check in the bank. I know you're supposed to order the filet, but I like my beef with a little more flavor, so I had the ribeye. Heidi had ordered a chunk of prime rib that appeared to have been sliced from the side of Babe the Blue Ox. We were already on our second bottle of malbec. I didn't worry about driving home, which was only blocks away. I was growing concerned about hoofing it, however.

"*Resort* security," I corrected. "A new hundred–fifty acre mixed recreational and hotel complex overlooking the crystal sands of Waikiki Beach. All inclusive, adults only, party-'til-you-drop central. He's in charge of the entire she-bang, security-wise."

"Adults-only," she said. "Guess no lost kids, then?"

"Absolutely no lost kids. Maybe a few lost marriages."

"Oh. It's *that* kind of resort."

"What happens in Waikiki stays in Waikiki," I told her. "Place like that, though, is a magnet for card sharps and conmen and thieves."

"Everyone has an angle."

"And they play them like mathematicians. Sonny has a good eye for lowlifes and ne'er-do-wells. He's going to stay extremely busy holding down the crime in paradise."

"Doesn't sound like a half-bad gig," she said. "We should visit. Frequently."

"Did I mention that, as Security Chief, Sonny can comp us a room?"

"But only when there isn't a murder to solve," she cautioned.

"Sweetie," I told her, "*Especially* when there is a murder to solve."

Heidi pouted briefly, and then brightened. "In that case, I'll be by the pool or in the bar whenever you're finished. Just don't get yourself killed or anything. I like to know who I'm sitting beside on the flight back."

I topped off her glass.

"Deal," I said.

THE END

ABOUT THE AUTHOR

Richard Helms is a retired college professor and forensic psychologist. He has been nominated eight times for the SMFS Derringer Award, winning it twice; seven times for the Private Eye Writers of America Shamus Award, with one win; twice for the ITW Thriller Award, with one win; four times for the Killer Nashville Silver Falchion Award with one win: and once for the Mystery Readers International Macavity Award. *Doctor Hate* is his twenty-first novel. He is a frequent contributor to *Ellery Queen Mystery Magazine*, along with other periodicals and short story anthologies, and his story *"See Humble and Die"* was included in Houghton-Mifflin-Harcourt's *Best American Mystery Stories 2020*. Mr. Helms is a former member of the Board of Directors of Mystery Writers of America, and the former president of the Southeast Regional Chapter of MWA. When not writing, Mr. Helms enjoys travel, gourmet cooking, simracing, rooting for his beloved Carolina Tar Heels and Carolina Panthers, and playing with his grandsons. Richard Helms and his wife Elaine live in Charlotte, North Carolina.

Made in United States
North Haven, CT
16 April 2022

18320459R00189